Navy Husband

DEBBIE MACOMBER

SILHOUETTE®

SPECIAL EDITION™

To Geri Krotow, Navy wife,
with appreciation for all her asssistance.
Dream big dreams, my friend.

*First published in Great Britain 2006
Silhouette Books, Eton House, 18-24 Paradise Road,
Richmond, Surrey TW9 1SR*

© Debbie Macomber 2005

*Standard ISBN 0 373 24693 5
Promotional ISBN 0 373 60479 3*

23-0806

*Printed and bound in Spain
by Litografía Rosés S.A., Barcelona*

DEBBIE MACOMBER

hails from the state of Washington. As a busy wife and mother of four, she strives to keep her family happy and healthy. As a prolific author of dozens of romance novels, she strives to keep her readers happy with each new book she writes.

Dear Friends,

Here it is—the very last book of my Navy series, written in the summer of 2004. A lot has changed since I wrote those first five books in the late 1980s and early nineties. There have been huge technological advances that affect our everyday lives—and life in the Navy, too.

Even after all these years, I'll never forget my first sight of an aircraft carrier when the *Nimitz* sailed into Sinclair Inlet that day in 1988. I still feel the excitement and joy experienced by the crowd of people waiting to see their loved ones. But I felt more than joy that day—I also felt pride and respect. All of those emotions led me to bring my hand to my heart and join in the singing of "God Bless America."

As you've probably figured out by now, I live in a Navy town. The Bremerton shipyard is directly across Sinclair Inlet from Port Orchard. Many of my neighbours are active or retired military families, and a number of the women who attend my local autographings are Navy wives. (I've even met a few Navy husbands!) I'm proud to be part of this community, proud to support our military and their families. We are the land of the free because of the brave, and I don't ever want to forget that.

Thank you for reading my books. Now sit back, put your feet up and enjoy *Navy Husband*.

Warmest regards,

Debbie Macomber

PS I love hearing from readers. You can reach me through my website, www.debbiemacomber.com (write your comments in the guest book) or write to me at PO Box 1458, Port Orchard, WA 98366,USA.

Chapter One

"This is a joke—right?" Shana Berrie said uncertainly as she talked to her older sister, Ali, on the phone. Ali was the sensible one in the family. She—unlike Shana—wouldn't have dreamed of packing up her entire life, buying a pizza and ice-cream parlor and starting over in a new city. Oh, no, only someone completely and utterly in need of a change—correction, a *drastic* change—would do something like that.

"I'm sorry, Shana, but you did agree to this parenting plan."

Her sister was a Navy nurse stationed in San Diego, and several years ago, when she'd asked Shana to look after her niece if necessary, Shana had immediately said yes. It had seemed an unlikely prospect at the time, but that was before her sister became a widow.

"I did, didn't I?" she muttered lamely as she stepped

around a cardboard box. Her rental house was cluttered with the makings of her new life and the remnants of her old.

"It isn't like I have any choice in the matter," Ali pointed out.

"I know." Pushing her thick, chestnut-colored hair away from her forehead, Shana leaned against the kitchen wall and slowly expelled her breath, hoping that would calm her pounding heart. "I said yes back then because you asked me to, but I don't know anything about kids."

"Jazmine's great," Ali assured her.

"I know, but—but…" she stammered. Shana wasn't sure how to explain. "The thing is, I'm at a turning point in my own life and I'm probably not the best person for Jazmine." Surely there was a relative on her brother-in-law's side. Someone else, *anyone* else would be better than Shana, who was starting a new career after suffering a major romantic breakup. At the moment, her life still felt disorganized. Chaotic. Add a recently bereaved nine-year-old to the mix, and she didn't know what might happen.

"This isn't a choose-your-time type of situation," Ali said. "I'm counting on you, and so is Jazmine."

Shana nibbled on her lower lip, trapped between her doubts and her obligation to her widowed sister. "I'll do it, of course, but I was just wondering if there was someone else…."

"There isn't," Ali said abruptly.

"Then it's me." Shana spoke with as much enthusiasm as she could muster, although she suspected it must sound pretty hollow. Shana hadn't had much experience as an aunt, but she was going to get her chance to learn.

She was about to become her niece's primary caregiver while her sister went out to sea on an aircraft carrier for a six-month deployment.

Shana truly hadn't expected this. When Ali filled out the "worldwide availability" form—with Shana's name—she'd explained it was so the Navy had documentation proving Jazmine would have someone to take care of her at all times, ensuring that Ali was combat-ready. It had seemed quite routine, more of a formality than a possibility—and of course, Peter was alive then.

Ali had been in the Navy for twelve years and had never pulled sea duty before now. She'd traveled around the world with her husband, a Navy pilot, and their daughter. Then, two years ago, Peter had been killed in a training accident and everything changed.

Things had changed in Shana's life, too, although not in the same unalterable and tragic way. Brad—Shana purposely put a halt to her thoughts. Brad was in the past. They were finished. Done. Kaput. She'd told her friends that she was so over him she had to force herself to remember his name. Who was he, again? *That* was how over him she was. Over. Over and out.

"I don't have much time," Ali was saying. "The *Woodrow Wilson*'s scheduled to leave soon. I'll fly Jazmine up this weekend but I won't be able to stay more than overnight."

Shana swallowed a protest. For reasons of national security, Shana realized her sister couldn't say any more about her schedule. But this weekend? She still had to finish unpacking. Furthermore, she'd only just started training with the former owners of her restaurant. Then it occurred to Shana that she might not be the only one upset about Ali's sudden deployment. She could only guess at her niece's reaction. "What does Jazmine have to say about all this?"

Ali's hesitation told Shana everything she needed to know. "Oh, great," she muttered under her breath. She remembered her own childhood and what her mother had termed her "attitude problem." Shana had plenty of that, all right, and most of it was bad. Dealing with Jazmine's moods would be payback, she supposed, for everything her poor mother had endured.

"To be honest, Jazmine isn't too excited about the move."

Who could blame her? The little girl barely knew Shana. The kid, a true child of the military, had lived on Whidbey Island in Washington State, then Italy and, following the accident that claimed her father's life, had been shuffled to San Diego, California. They'd just settled into their Navy housing, and now they were about to leave that. In her nine years Jazmine had been moved from country to country, lost her father, and now her mother was shipping out for six long months. If that wasn't enough, the poor kid was being foisted on Shana. No wonder she wasn't thrilled.

"We'll be fine," Shana murmured, doing her best to sound positive. She didn't know who she was kidding. Certainly not her sister—and not herself, either. This was going to be another in a long line of recent disasters, or life-changing events, as she preferred to call them.

"So it's true you and Brad split up?" Ali asked with a degree of delicacy. She'd obviously been warned against bringing up his name.

"Brad?" Shana repeated as if she had no idea who her sister was talking about. "Oh, you mean Brad Moore.

Yes, it's over. We were finished quite a while ago, but either he forgot to tell me or I just wasn't paying attention."

"I'm so sorry," Ali said.

The last thing Shana wanted was Ali's sympathy. "Don't worry, I've rebounded. Everything's great. My life is fabulous, or it will be in short order. I've got everything under control." Shana said all of this without taking a breath. If she said it often enough, she might actually start to believe it.

"When Mom told me that you'd decided to leave Portland and move to Seattle, I thought it was job-related at first. You never said a word." She paused. "Did you move all those plants, too? You must have about a thousand."

Shana laughed. "Hardly. But yes, I did. Moving was…a spontaneous decision." That was putting it mildly. One weekend Shana had driven to Seattle to get away and to consider her relationship with Brad. She'd finally realized that it wasn't going anywhere. For five years they'd been talking marriage. Wrong. *She'd* been talking marriage. Brad had managed to string her along with just enough interest to placate her. And she'd let him until…

Unexpectedly, Shana had stumbled on Brad having lunch with a business associate. This so-called associate just happened to be a willowy blonde with a figure that would stop a freight train. It was a business lunch, he'd claimed later, when Shana confronted him.

Yeah, sure—monkey business. Shana could be dense at times but she wasn't blind, and she recognized this so-called associate as someone Brad had once introduced as Sylvia, an old flame. Apparently those embers were still very much alive and growing hotter by the minute, because as Shana watched, they'd exchanged a lengthy kiss in the parking lot and drove off together. She was embarrassed to admit she'd followed them. It didn't take her long to see where they were headed. Brad's town house—and she didn't think they were there to discuss contracts or fire codes.

Even when confronted, Brad insisted his lunch date was a client. Any resemblance his associate had to Sylvia was purely coincidental. The more he defended himself, the more defensive he got, complaining that Shana was acting like a jealous shrew. He'd been outraged that she'd question his faithfulness when *she* was the one so often away, working as a sales rep for a large pharmaceutical company. He'd been so convincing that—just for a moment—she'd wondered if she might've been wrong. Only when she mentioned that she'd followed them to his town house did Brad show any hint of guilt or regret.

He'd glanced away then, and the righteous indignation had been replaced by a look of such sadness she had to resist the urge to comfort him. He was sorry, he'd said, so sorry. It had been a fling; it meant nothing. He couldn't lose her. Shana was his life, the woman he intended to marry, the mother of his unborn children.

For a few days, he'd actually swayed her. Needing to sort out her feelings, Shana had driven to Seattle the next weekend. After five years with Brad she felt she knew him, but it now seemed quite clear that she didn't. He wanted her back, he told her over and over. He was willing to do whatever it took to reconcile, to make this up to her. He suggested counseling, agreed to therapy, anything but losing her.

That weekend, Shana had engaged in some painful

self-examination. She desperately wanted to believe the afternoon rendezvous with Sylvia was a onetime thing, but her head told her it wasn't and that they'd been involved for months—or more.

It was while she sat in Lincoln Park in West Seattle, analyzing the last five years, that she concluded there was no going back. Her trust had been destroyed. She couldn't build a life with Brad after this. In truth, their relationship had dead-ended three years ago. Maybe sooner; she could no longer tell. What Shana did recognize was that she'd been so caught up in loving Brad that she'd refused to see the signs.

"I was feeling pretty miserable," Shana admitted to her sister. Wretched was a more accurate description, but she didn't want to sound melodramatic. "I sat in that park in West Seattle, thinking."

"In West Seattle? How'd you get there?"

Shana sighed loudly. "I took a wrong turn when I was trying to find the freeway."

Ali laughed. "I should have guessed."

"I ended up on this bridge and there wasn't anyplace to turn around, so I followed the road, which led to a wonderful waterfront park."

"The ice-cream parlor's in the park?"

"No, it's across the street. You know me and maple-nut ice cream. It's the ultimate comfort food." She tried to make a joke of it, but at the time she'd felt there wasn't enough maple-nut ice cream in the world to see her through this misery.

"Brad drove you to maple nut?"

Shana snickered at Ali's exaggerated horror. After her decision to break off the relationship, she'd grown angry. Okay, furious. She wanted out of this relationship, completely out, and living in the same city made that difficult.

"Actually, West Seattle is a charming little community. The ice-cream parlor had a For Sale sign in the window and I got to talking to the owners. They're an older couple, sweet as can be and planning to retire. As I sat there, I thought it must be a nice place to work. How could anyone be unhappy surrounded by ice cream and pizza?"

"So you *bought* it? Shana, for heaven's sake, what do you know about running any kind of restaurant?"

"Not much," she said, "but I've worked in sales and with people all these years. I was ready for a break, and this seemed practically fated."

"But how could you afford to buy an established business?"

Shana had an answer for that, too. "I had a chunk of cash in savings." The money had originally been set aside for her wedding. Saving a hundred dollars a month and investing it carefully, she'd managed to double her money. Just then, she couldn't think of a better way to spend it. Buying this business was impulsive and irrational but despite everything, it felt…right.

That Sunday in the park she'd admitted there would be no wedding, no honeymoon with Brad. Shana drew in her breath. She refused to think about it anymore. She'd entered a new phase of her life.

"It's a cute place. You'll like it," she murmured. She had lots of ideas for fixing it up, making it *hers*. The Olsens had promised to help transfer ownership as seamlessly as possible.

"You rented a house?"

"That very same Sunday." Once she'd made her decision, Shana had been on a mission and there was no stopping her. As luck would have it, there was a house two streets over that had just been vacated. The owner had recently painted it and installed new carpeting. Shana had taken one look around the 1950s-style bungalow with its small front porch and brick fireplace and declared it perfect. She'd given the rental agent a check immediately. Then she drove home, wrote a letter resigning her job—and phoned Brad. That conversation had been short, sweet and utterly satisfying.

"Making a move like this couldn't have been easy," Ali commiserated.

"You wouldn't believe how easy it was," Shana said gleefully. "I suppose you're curious about what Brad had to say." She was dying to tell her.

"Well…"

"I called him," Shana said without waiting for Ali to respond, "and naturally he wanted to know where I'd been all weekend."

"You told him?"

Shana grinned. "I couldn't get a word in edgewise. He was pretty upset. He told me how worried he was, and how he'd spent the entire weekend calling me. He was afraid of what I might've done. As if I'd do something lethal over *him*," she scoffed. Shana suspected that his concern was all for show, but none of that mattered now. "When he cooled down, I calmly explained that I'd gone for a drive."

"A three-day drive," Ali inserted.

"Right. Well, he got huffy, saying the least I could've done was let him know I'd made plans." What came next was the best part. "So I told him I'd made plans for the rest of my life and they didn't include him."

Ali giggled and it sounded exactly the way it had

when they were girls, sharing a bedroom. "What did he say then?"

"I don't know. I hung up and started packing stuff in my apartment."

"Didn't he try to phone you back?"

"Not for the first couple of days. He e-mailed me on the third day and I immediately put a block on his name." That must have infuriated him—not that Shana cared. Well, she did, a little. Okay, more than a little. Unfortunately she didn't have the satisfaction of knowing what his reaction had been. In the past, she'd always been the one who patched any rift. That was her problem; she couldn't stand conflict, so she'd done all the compromising and conciliating. Over the course of their relationship, Brad had come to expect her to make the first move. Well, no longer. She was finished. Brad Moore was history.

Instead of kicking herself for taking so long to see the light, she was moving ahead, starting over…and, to be on the safe side, giving up on men and relationships. At twenty-eight, she'd had her fill. Men weren't worth the effort and the grief.

"I never was that fond of Brad," Ali confessed.

"You might've said something." Shana realized her tone was a little annoyed. In the five years she'd dated Brad, there'd certainly been opportunities for Ali to share her opinion.

"How could I? We just met once, and you seemed so keen on him."

"If you'd stayed in one place longer, we might've gotten together more often."

Ali's sigh drifted over the phone. "That's what happens when you're in the Navy. They own your life. Now honestly, are you all right?"

Shana paused to consider the question. A second later, she gave Ali her answer. "Honestly? I feel great, and that's the truth. Yes, this breakup hurt, but mostly I was angry with myself for not waking up sooner. I feel *fabulous*. It's as if I've been released from a spell. I've got a whole new attitude toward men."

Her sister didn't say anything for a moment. "You might *think* you're fine, but there's a chance you're not totally over Brad."

"What do you mean?"

Again her sister hesitated. "I remember what it was like after Peter died. The shock and grief were overwhelming at first. I walked around in a fog for weeks."

"This is different," Shana insisted. "It's less…important."

"It is and it isn't," Ali fired right back.

"But you feel better now, don't you?"

"Yes. One day, out of the blue, I discovered I could smile again. I could function. I had to. My daughter needed me. My patients needed me. I'll always love Peter, though." Her voice wavered but eventually regained strength.

"I'll always love Peter, too," Shana said, swallowing hard. "He was one of a kind." Her brother-in-law had been a loving husband and father, and her heart ached for her sister even now. The situation with Brad didn't compare.

"I'll give you my flight information for this weekend," Ali said, changing the subject.

Shana had nearly forgotten that she was about to become a substitute mother. "Oh, yeah. Let me find a pen." Scrabbling through her purse, she dug one up and found a crumpled receipt she'd stuffed in there. Good—she could write on the back.

She was looking forward to some time with her sister. They saw each other so rarely, thanks to Ali's career. This upcoming visit would be a brief one, but Shana hadn't seen Ali—and Jazmine—since the funeral.

"You and Jazmine will do just fine," Ali said warmly. "Jazmine's a great kid, but be warned. She's nine going on sixteen."

"In what way?"

"Because she's an only child, she's rather…precocious. For instance, she's reading at ninth-grade level. And the music she likes is sort of—well, you'll see."

"Thanks for warning me."

"I'm sure this'll be easy for you."

Shana had her doubts. "If I remember correctly, that was what you told me when I asked if I could fly off the top bunk."

"What did I know? I was only six," Ali reminded her. "You've never forgiven me for that, have you?"

"I still remember how much it hurt to have the wind knocked out of me." It felt the same way now. Despite the assurances she so freely handed out, Shana was still struggling to recover her equilibrium—to reinvent her life on new terms. No Brad, no steady paycheck, no familiar Portland neighborhood. Now, her niece was about to complicate the situation. The next six months should be very interesting, she thought. Very interesting indeed.

She vaguely recalled an old Chinese saying, something about living in interesting times. Unfortunately, she also recalled that it was intended as a curse, not a blessing.

Chapter Two

Alison Karas couldn't help being concerned about leaving her nine-year-old daughter with her sister, Shana. This wasn't a good time in Jazmine's life, nor was it particularly opportune for Shana. Her sister *sounded* strong and confident, but Ali suspected otherwise. Despite Shana's reassurances, she'd been badly shaken by her breakup with Brad, even though she'd initiated it. Jazmine hadn't taken the news of this deployment well, and was reluctant to leave her newfound friends behind and move to Seattle.

But Ali really had no other option. Ideally, Jazmine would go to either set of grandparents, but in this case that wouldn't work. After the sudden loss of her father ten years earlier, her mother hadn't done well. She'd never recovered emotionally and was incapable of dealing with the demands of a young girl. Peter had been an only child and his parents had divorced when he was young. Both had gone on to other marriages and other children. Neither set of paternal grandparents had shown any great interest in Jazmine.

Jazmine wandered into Ali's room just then and flopped down on the bed with all the enthusiasm of a slug.

"Are you packed?" Ali asked, her own suitcase open on the opposite end of the bed.

"No," her daughter muttered. "This whole move is crap."

"Jazmine, watch your mouth!" Ali refused to get into an argument with a nine-year-old. The truth was, she'd rather not ship out, either, but for Jazmine's sake she put on a good front. This was the most difficult aspect of her life in the Navy. She was a widow and a mother, but she was also a Navy nurse, and her responsibilities in that regard were unavoidable. That was made abundantly clear the day she accepted her commission. When the Navy called, she answered. In fact, she wouldn't have minded six months at sea except for her daughter.

"Uncle Adam lives in the Seattle area," Ali reminded her. She'd been saving that tidbit, hoping the news would make her daughter feel more positive about this most recent upheaval in their lives.

"He's in Everett," Jazmine said, her voice apathetic.

"I understand that's only thirty or forty minutes from Seattle."

"It is?"

Her daughter revealed her first spark of interest since they'd learned of the transfer. "Does he know we're coming?" She sat upright, eager now.

"Not yet." Busy as she'd been, Ali hadn't told Adam

Kennedy—her husband's best friend and Jazz's godfather—that Jazmine would soon be living in Seattle.

"Then we *have* to tell him!"

"We will, all in due course," Ali assured her.

"Do it now." Her daughter leaped off the bed,
sprinted into the living room and came back with the
portable phone.

"I don't have his number." Ali hadn't been thinking
clearly; their phone directory had already been packed
away and she simply didn't have time to search for it.

"I do." Once more her daughter made a mad dash out
of the bedroom, returning a moment later. Breathless,
Jazmine handed Ali a tidy slip of paper.

Ali unfolded it curiously and saw a phone number
written by an adult hand.

"Uncle Adam sent it to me," Jazmine explained. "He
told me I could call him whenever I needed to talk. He
said it didn't matter what time of day or night I phoned,
so call him, Mom. This is *important.*"

Ali resisted the urge to find out if her daughter had
taken advantage of Adam's offer before now and decided
she probably had. For Jazmine, it was as if the sun rose
and set on Peter's friend. Lieutenant Commander Adam
Kennedy had been a support to both of them since the accident that had abruptly taken Peter out of their lives.

It sounded so cut and dried to say a computer had
malfunctioned aboard Peter's F/A-18. He hadn't had a
chance to recover before the jet slammed into the
ground. He'd died instantly, his life snuffed out in mere
seconds. That was two years ago now, two very long
years, and every day since, Peter had been with her. Her
first thought was always of him and his image was the
last one her mind released before she went to sleep at

night. He was part of her. She saw him in Jazmine's smile, in the three little lines that formed between the girl's eyebrows when she frowned. Peter had done that, too. And their eyes were the exact same shade of brownish green.

As an SMO, or senior medical officer, Ali was familiar with death. What she didn't know was how to deal with the aftermath of it. She still struggled and, as a result, she understood her sister's pain. Yes, Shana's breakup with Brad was different, and of a lesser magnitude, but it was a loss. In ending her relationship with him, Shana was also giving up a dream, one she'd held and cherished for five years. She was adjusting to a new version of her life and her future. Shana had flippantly dismissed any doubts or regrets about the breakup. Those would come later, like a sneak attack—probably when Shana least expected it. They had with Ali.

"Mom," Jazmine cried, exasperated. "Dial!"

"Oh, sorry," Ali murmured, punching out the number. An answering machine came on almost immediately.

"He isn't there?" Jazmine asked, studying her. She didn't hide her disappointment. It was doom and gloom all over again as she threw herself backward onto the bed, arms spread-eagled.

Ali left a message and asked him to get in touch.

"When do you think he'll call?" Jazmine demanded impatiently.

"I don't know, but I'll make sure we get a chance to see him if it's possible."

"Of *course* it's possible," Jazmine argued. "He'll want to see me. And you, too."

Ali shrugged. "He might not be back by the time I need to fly out, but you'll see him, don't worry."

Jazmine wouldn't look at her. Instead she stared morosely at the ceiling, as if she didn't have a friend in the world. The kid had moved any number of times and had always been a good sport about it, until now. Ali didn't blame her for being upset, but there wasn't anything she could do to change her orders.

"You'll love living with your aunt Shana," Alison said, trying a new tactic. "Did I tell you she has an ice-cream parlor? How much fun is that?"

Jazmine wasn't impressed. "I don't really know her."

"This will be your opportunity to bond."

Jazmine sighed. "I don't want to bond with her."

"You will eventually," Ali said with forced brightness. Jazmine wasn't fooled.

"I'm not glue, you know."

Alison held back a smile. "We both need to make the best of this, Jazz. I don't want to leave you any more than you want me to go."

Her daughter scrambled to a sitting position. As her shoulders slumped, she nodded. "I know."

"Your aunt Shana loves you."

"Yippee, skippy."

Alison tried again. "The ice-cream parlor is directly across the street from the park."

"Yippee."

"Jazmine!"

"I know, I know."

Ali wrapped one arm around the girl's shoulders. "The months will fly by. You'll see."

Jazmine shook her head. "No, they won't," she said adamantly, "and I have to change schools again. I hate that."

Changing schools, especially this late in the year,

would be difficult. In a few weeks, depending on the Seattle schedule, classes would be dismissed for the summer. Ali kissed the top of Jazmine's head and closed her eyes. She had the distinct feeling her daughter was right. The next six months wouldn't fly, they'd crawl. For all three of them...

Shana wanted children, someday, when the time was right. But she'd assumed she'd take on the role of motherhood the way everyone else did. She'd start with an infant and sort of grow into it—ease into being a parent gradually, learning as she went. Instead, she was about to get a crash course. She wondered if there were manuals to help with this kind of situation.

Pacing her living room, she paused long enough to check out the spare bedroom one last time. She'd added some welcoming touches for Jazmine's benefit and hoped the stuffed teddy bear would appeal to her niece. Girls of any age liked stuffed animals, didn't they? The bedspread, a fetching shade of pink with big white daisies, was new, as was the matching pink throw rug. She just hoped Jazmine would recognize that she was trying to make this work.

She wanted Jazmine to know she was willing to make an effort if the girl would meet her halfway. Still, Shana didn't have a good feeling about it.

Her suspicions proved correct. When Ali arrived, it was immediately apparent that Jazmine wanted nothing to do with her aunt Shana. The nine-year-old was dressed in faded green fatigues and a camouflage army-green T-shirt. She sat on the sofa with a sullen look that discouraged conversation. Her long dark hair fell across her face. When she wasn't glaring at Shana, she stared at the carpet as if inspecting it for loose fibers.

"I can't tell you how good it is to see you," Ali told Shana, turning to her daughter, obviously expecting Jazmine to echo the sentiment. The girl didn't.

Shana moved into the kitchen, hoping for a private word with her sister. They hadn't always been close. All through high school, they'd competed with each other. Ali had been the more academic of the two, while Shana had excelled in sports. From their father, a family physician, they'd both inherited a love of science and medicine. He'd died suddenly of a heart attack when Shana was twenty.

Within months, their lives were turned upside down. Their mother fell to pieces but by that time, Ali was in the Navy. Luckily, Shana was able to stay close to home and look after their mom, handle the legal paperwork and deal with the insurance, retirement funds and other responsibilities. Shana had attended college classes part-time and kept the household going. At twenty-two, she was hired by one of the up-and-coming pharmaceutical companies as a sales rep. The job suited her. Having spent a good part of her life around medical professionals, she was comfortable in that atmosphere. She was friendly and personable, well-liked by clients and colleagues. Within a few years, she'd risen to top sales representative in her division. The company had been sorry to see her go and had offered an impressive bonus to persuade her to stay. But Shana was ready for a change, in more ways than one.

The last time the sisters had been together was at Peter's funeral. Shortly afterward, Ali had returned to Italy. Although she could have taken an assignment back in

the States, Ali chose to finish her tour in Europe. As
much as possible, she'd told Shana, she wanted Jazmine
to remain in a familiar environment. A few months ago,
she'd been transferred to San Diego, but no one had expected her to be stationed aboard the *Woodrow Wilson,*
the newest and largest of the Navy's aircraft carriers. According to her sister, this was a once-in-a-career assignment. Maybe, but in Shana's opinion, the Navy had a
lousy sense of timing.

"Jazmine doesn't seem happy about being here,"
Shana commented when they were out of earshot. She
understood how the girl felt. The poor kid had enough
turmoil in her life without having her mother disappear
for six months.

"She'll be fine." Ali cast an anxious glance toward
the living room as Shana took three sodas from the
refrigerator.

"Sure she will," Shana agreed, "but will I?"

Ali bit her lower lip and looked guilty. "There isn't
anyone else."

"I know. These next six months will give Jazmine and
me a chance to know each other," Shana announced,
stepping into the living room and offering Jazmine a
soda. "Isn't that right?"

The girl stared at the can as if it held nerve gas. "I
don't want to live with you."

Well, surprise, surprise. Shana would never have
guessed that.

"Jazmine!"

"No," Shana said, stopping her sister from chastis-
ing the girl. "We should be honest with one another."
She put down Jazmine's drink and sat on the opposite
end of the sofa, dangling her own pop can in both hands.

"This is going to be an experience for me, too. I haven't been around kids your age all that much."

"I can tell." Jazmine frowned at the open door to her bedroom. "I hate pink."

Shana had been afraid of that. "We can take it back and exchange it for something you like."

"Where'd you get it? Barbies R Us?"

Shana laughed; the kid was witty. "Close, but we can check out the Army surplus store if you prefer."

This comment warranted a half smile from Jazmine.

"We'll manage," Shana said with what she hoped sounded like confidence. "I realize I've got a lot to learn."

"No kidding."

"Jazmine," Ali snapped in frustration, "the least you can do is try. Give your aunt credit for making an effort. You can do the same."

"I am trying," the girl snapped in return. "A pink bedroom and a teddy bear? Oh, puleeeze! She's treating me like I'm in kindergarten instead of fourth grade."

Shana had barely started this new venture and already she'd failed miserably. "We can exchange the bear, too," she suggested. "Army surplus again?"

Her second attempt at being accommodating was less appreciated than the first. This time Jazmine didn't even crack a smile.

Ali sat in the space between Shana and Jazmine and threw her arms over their shoulders. "If I've learned anything in the last few years, it's that women have to stick together. I can't be with you, Jazz. That's all there is to it. I'm sorry, I wish things were different, but they aren't. If you want, at the end of this deployment, I'll resign my commission."

Jazmine's head rose abruptly. "You'd leave the Navy?"

Ali nodded. This was as much a surprise to Shana as it was to her niece. From all indications, Ali loved military life and had fit into it with comfort and ease.

"Now that your dad's gone, my life isn't the same anymore," Ali continued. "I'm your mother and you're far more important to me than any career, Navy or not. I won't leave you again, Jazmine, and that's a promise."

At those words the girl burst into tears. Embarrassed, she hid her face in both hands, her shoulders shaking as Ali hugged her.

Ali seemed to be trying not to weep, but Shana had no such compunction. Tears slipped down her cheeks.

It would be so good to have her sister back again. If she had any say in the matter, Ali would move to Seattle so the two of them could be closer.

"If you get out of the Navy, does that mean you'll marry Uncle Adam?" Jazmine asked with the excitement of a kid who's just learned she's about to receive the best gift of her life.

"Who's Uncle Adam?" Did this mean her sister had managed to find *two* husbands while Shana had yet to find one? Ah, the old competitive urge was back in full swing.

"He was one of my dad's best friends," Jazmine supplied with more enthusiasm than she'd shown since she'd arrived. "He's cute and funny and I think Mom should marry him."

Raising one brow, Shana turned to her sister for an explanation. Ali had never mentioned anyone named Adam.

"Uncle Adam is stationed in Everett. That's close to here, right?" Jazmine demanded, looking to Shana for the answer.

"It's a bit of a drive." She wasn't entirely sure, never

having made the trip north of Seattle herself. "Less than an hour, I'd guess."

"Uncle Adam will want to visit once he learns I'm here."

"I'm sure he will," Ali murmured, pressing her daughter's head against her shoulder.

"You like this guy?" Shana asked her. Ali was decidedly closemouthed about him, which implied that she had some feelings for this friend of Peter's.

"Of course Mom likes him," Jazmine said when her mother didn't respond. "So do I. He's totally *fabulous.*"

Ali met Shana's gaze and shrugged.

"Another pilot?" Shana murmured.

She shook her head. "He's a Supply Officer. You'll like him," her sister was quick to say, as if this man might interest her romantically. No way. Shana had sworn off men and she was serious about that.

"He said I can talk to him anytime I want," Jazmine went on. "I can phone him, can't I?"

"Of course you can." Shana was more curious than ever about this man her sister didn't want to discuss.

Shana turned to gaze at Ali, silently pleading for more information. Her sister ignored her, which was infuriating. Clearly, Adam had already won over her niece; he must be the kind of guy who shopped at the army surplus store.

Chapter Three

First thing Monday morning, Shana drove Jazmine to Lewis and Clark Elementary School to enroll her. Shana had to admit her stomach was in knots. The school yard was jammed with kids, and a string of vehicles queued in front, taking turns dropping off students. Big yellow school buses belched out diesel fumes as they lumbered toward the parking lot behind the building.

Shana was fortunate to find an empty parking space. She accompanied Jazmine into the building, although the girl walked ahead of her—just far enough to suggest the two of them weren't together.

The noise level inside the school reminded her of a rock concert and Shana felt the beginnings of a headache. Or maybe it was caused by all those students gathered in one place, staring at Jazmine and her.

The school bell rang and like magic, the halls emptied. Within seconds everyone disappeared behind various doors and silence descended. Ah, the power of a bell. It was as if she were Moses, and the Red Sea had parted so she could find her way to the Promised Land, or in this case, The Office.

Wordlessly Shana and Jazmine followed the signs to the principal's domain. Jazmine was outwardly calm. She gave no sign of being ill at ease. Unlike Shana, who was on the verge of chewing off every fingernail she owned.

"This is no big deal," Jazmine assured her, shifting the backpack she carried. It was the size one might take on a trek through the Himalayas. "I've done this plenty of times."

"I don't feel good just leaving you here." They'd had all of one day together and while it was uncomfortable for them both, it hadn't been nearly as bad as Shana had feared. It hadn't been good, either.

When they took Ali to the airport, Shana had been the one in tears. Mother and daughter had hugged for an extra-long moment and then Ali was gone. It was Shana who did all the talking on the drive home. As soon as they were back at the rental house, Jazmine disappeared inside her bedroom and didn't open the door for hours.

Dinner had been a series of attempts on Shana's part to start a conversation, but her questions were met with either a grunt or a one-word reply. Shana got the message. After the first ten minutes, she said nothing. And *nothing* was what Jazmine seemed to appreciate most. They maintained an awkward silence and at the end of the meal, Jazmine delivered her plate to the kitchen, rinsed it off, stuck it in the dishwasher and returned to her room. The door closed and Shana hadn't seen her again until this morning. Apparently kids this age treasured their privacy. Point taken. Lesson learned.

"This must be it," Shana said, pointing at the door marked *Office*.

Jazmine murmured something unintelligible, shrugging off the backpack and letting the straps slip down her arms. Shana couldn't imagine what she had in that monstrosity, but apparently it was as valuable to the child as Shana's purse was to her.

"I was thinking you might want to wait a bit, you know," Shana suggested, stammering, unable to identify her misgivings. "Not do this right away, I mean." The students she saw in the hallway didn't look particularly friendly. Jazmine was only nine, for heaven's sake, and her mother was headed out to sea for half a year. Maybe she should homeschool her. Shana considered that option for all of half a second. First, it wouldn't be home school; it would be ice-cream parlor school. The authorities would love that. And second, Shana was completely unqualified to teach her anything.

"I'll be all right," Jazmine said just loudly enough for Shana to hear.

Maybe so, but Shana wasn't completely convinced *she* would be. This guardianship thing was even harder than it sounded. The thought of leaving her niece here actually made her feel ill.

Jazmine's eyes narrowed accusingly. "I'm not a kid, you know."

So nine-year-olds weren't kids anymore? Could've fooled Shana, but rather than argue, she let the comment slide.

Enrolling Jazmine turned out to be surprisingly easy. After Shana completed a couple of forms and handed over a copy of her guardianship papers, it was done. Jazmine was led out of the office and into a classroom. Shana watched her go, forcing herself not to follow like a much-loved golden retriever.

"It's your first time as a guardian?" the school secretary asked.

Shana nodded. "Jazmine's been through a lot." She resisted the urge to mention Peter's death and the fact that Ali was out at sea. Instinctively she realized that the less anyone knew about these things, the better for Jazmine.

"She'll fit right in," the secretary assured her.

"I hope so." But Shana wasn't sure that was true. There were only a few weeks left of the school year. Just when Jazmine had managed to adjust, it would be time for summer break. And what would Shana do with her then? It was a question she couldn't answer. Not yet, anyway.

With reluctance she walked back to her parked car and drove to Olsen's Ice Cream and Pizza Parlor. She'd thought about changing the name, but the restaurant had been called this for the last thirty years. A new name might actually be a disadvantage, so she'd decided to keep everything the same for now.

Shana's day went smoothly after her visit to the school. She was on her own now, her training with the Olsens finished. They insisted the secret to their pizza was the tomato sauce, made from their special recipe. That recipe had been kept secret for over thirty years. Only when the final papers had been signed was Shana allowed to have the recipe, which to her untrained eye looked fairly unspectacular. She was almost sure her mother used to make something similar for spaghetti and had gotten the recipe out of a "Dear Abby" column years ago.

There was a huge mixing machine and, following the Olsens' example, she went into the shop each morning to mix up a batch of dough and let it rise. Once the dough had risen, it was put in the refrigerator, awaiting the day's pizza orders. The restaurant opened at eleven and did a brisk lunch trade. How much or how little dough to make was complete guesswork. Shana's biggest fear was that she'd run short. As a consequence she usually mixed too much. But she was learning.

At three o'clock, Shana found herself watching for the school bus. Jazmine was to be dropped off in front of the ice-cream parlor. From noon on, she'd constantly checked the time, wondering and worrying about her niece. The elementary students she'd seen looked like a rough crowd—okay, maybe not the first- and second-graders, but the ones in the fifth and sixth grades, who were giants compared to Jazmine. Shana just hoped the girl could hold her own.

Business was constant—people waiting to catch ferries, high-school students, retired folk, tourists. Shana planned to hire a part-time employee soon. Another idea she had was to introduce soup to the menu. She'd already experimented with a number of mixes, both liquid and dry, and hadn't found anything that impressed her. Shana was leaning toward making her own from scratch but her experience in cooking large batches was limited.

A bus rolled into view and Shana instantly went on alert. Sure enough, Jazmine stepped off, wearing a frown, and marched inside. Without a word to Shana, she slid into a booth.

"Well," Shana said, unable to disguise her anxiety, "how was it?"

Jazmine shrugged.

"Oh." Her niece wasn't exactly forthcoming with details. Thinking fast, Shana asked the questions her mother had bombarded her with every day after school. "What did you learn? Anything interesting?"

Jazmine shook her head.

"Did you make any new friends?"

Jazmine scowled up at her. "No."

That was said emphatically enough for Shana to surmise that things hadn't gone well. "I see." Glancing over her shoulder, Shana sighed. "Are you hungry? I could make you a pizza."

"No, thanks."

The bell above the door rang and a customer entered, moving directly to the ice-cream case. Shana slipped behind the counter and waited patiently until the woman had made her selection. As she scooped chocolate chip–mint ice cream into a waffle cone, she realized something was different about Jazmine. Not until her customer left did she figure out what it was.

"Jazz," she said, startled, "where's your backpack?"

Her niece didn't answer.

"Did you forget it at school? We could run by to pick it up if you want." Not until the parlor closed at six, but she didn't mention that. During the summer it wouldn't be until eight o'clock; she didn't mention that, either.

Jazmine scowled even more ferociously.

Shana hadn't known how much fury a nine-year-old girl's eyes could convey. Her niece's anger seemed to be focused solely on Shana. The unfairness of it struck her, but any attempt at conversation was instantly blocked.

It was obvious that someone had taken the backpack from Jazmine. No wonder the girl wasn't in a happy frame of mind.

Feeling wretched and helpless, Shana slid into the booth across from her niece. She didn't say anything for several minutes, then gently squeezed Jazmine's hand. "I am so sorry."

Jazmine shrugged as if it was no big thing, but it was and Shana felt at a loss. Without her niece's knowing, she'd speak to the principal in the morning and see what could be done. She guessed it'd happened on the bus or off school grounds.

"Can I use your phone?" Jazmine asked.

"Of course."

Jazmine's eyes fleetingly met hers as she pulled a piece of paper from her hip pocket. "It's long distance."

"You're not calling Paris, are you?"

The question evoked an almost-smile. "No."

"Sure, go ahead." Shana gestured toward the phone on the back wall in the kitchen.

Jazmine thanked her with a faint smile. This counted as profuse appreciation and Shana was nearly overwhelmed by gratitude. Despite their shaky beginning she was starting to reach this kid.

"I'm phoning my uncle Adam," Jazmine announced. "He'll know what to do."

This uncle Adam seemed to have all the answers. She hadn't even met him and already she didn't like him. No one could be that perfect.

On Monday afternoon, Adam Kennedy opened the door to his apartment near Everett Naval Station, glad to be home. He'd just been released from the naval hospital, where he'd recently undergone rotator cuff surgery. His shoulder throbbed and he felt so light-headed he had to brace his hand against the wall in order to steady himself. He'd be fine in a couple of days, but at the moment he was still shaky.

The apartment was dark with the drapes pulled, but he didn't have the energy to walk across the room and open them.

It wouldn't be like this if he had a wife, who'd be able to look after him while he felt so weak. This wasn't the first time that thought had occurred to Adam. He'd never intended to be a thirty-two-year-old bachelor.

Adam sank into his favorite chair and winced at the pain that shot down his arm. Leaning his head back against the cushion, he closed his eyes and envisioned what his life would be like if he was married. A wife would be fussing over him now, acting concerned and looking for ways to make him comfortable. Granted, if comfort was all he wanted, he could pay for it. A wife— well, having a wife meant companionship and sharing things. Like a bed… It also involved that frightening word, *love*.

If he was married now, she'd be asking how he felt and bringing him tea and *caring* about him. The fantasy filled his mind and he found himself smiling. What he needed was the *right* woman. His track record in that department left a great deal to be desired.

He'd started out fine. When he graduated from college he'd been engaged, but while he was in Officer Candidate School, Melanie had a sudden change of heart. Actually, she still wanted to get married, just not to him. The tearful scene in which she confessed that she'd fallen in love with someone else wasn't a memory he wanted to reminisce over, especially now. Suffice it to say, his ego had taken a major beating. In the long run, though, Melanie wasn't that great a loss. If she had a roving eye this early in their relationship, it didn't bode well for the lengthy separations a Navy career would demand of their marriage.

The thing was, Adam wanted children. One of his proudest moments was when Peter had asked him to be Jazmine's godfather. He took his duties seriously and loved that little girl, and he'd felt especially protective of her since his friend's death. He hadn't heard from her in a while and wondered how she was doing after the recent move to San Diego. He'd have to get in touch with her soon.

Adam had envied Peter his marriage. He'd never seen two people more in love with each other or better suited. They were about as perfect a match as possible. Adam suspected that fact had been a detriment to him in his own quest for a relationship. He kept looking for a woman as well suited to him as Ali had been to his friend. If such a woman existed, Adam hadn't found her, and he'd about given up. It wasn't Ali he wanted, but a woman who was his equal in all the ways Ali had been Peter's. A woman with brains and courage and heart. At this stage he'd take two out of three. Ali had brought out the best in Peter; she'd made a good man better.

A sense of sadness came over him as he thought about Peter. Adam had a couple of younger brothers, Sam and Doug, and the three of them were close, but Peter and Adam had been even closer. They'd met in OCS, Officer Candidate School, kept in contact afterward and later were stationed together in Italy. During weekend holidays, Peter and Ali had him over for countless dinners. The three of them had sat on their balcony in the Italian countryside drinking wine and talking well into the night. Those were some of the happiest memories of his life.

Then Peter had been killed. Adam had been a witness to the accident that claimed his best friend's life. He still had nightmares about it and experienced the same rush of horror, anger, frustration he'd felt at the time. He'd gone with the Casualty Assistance Counseling Officer to tell Ali that her husband was dead. In his heart, he'd promised Peter that he'd look out for both Ali and Jazz but the Navy hadn't made it easy.

Ali was currently stationed at the hospital in San Diego and he was in Everett. He phoned at least once a month to check up on them and Jazmine called him every now and then when she needed to talk. He always enjoyed their conversations. Peter would be proud of both the women in his life, he mused. Jazmine was a great kid and Ali was a wonderful mother.

Adam noticed the blinking light on his answering machine. He knew there were more messages than he had the patience or endurance to deal with just yet. He'd leave it until morning when he had a fresh supply of energy.

He sighed. He wasn't used to feeling like this—despondent and weary. Coming home to an empty apartment underlined a truth he didn't want to acknowledge. Lieutenant Commander Adam Kennedy was lonely.

He stared blankly across the room, half toying with the notion of a romantic relationship with Ali. It didn't take him more than a second to realize it wouldn't work. He loved Ali—like a sister. Try as he might, he couldn't seem to view her as a marriage prospect. She was his best friend's widow, a woman he admired, a woman he thought of as family.

Yet…he wanted what she'd had, what she and Peter had shared, and the deep contentment their marriage had brought them.

By morning, he would've forgotten all these yearnings, he told himself. He'd lived alone so long now that he should certainly be accustomed to his own company. When he was at sea, it was a different story, since he was constantly surrounded by others. As a Supply Officer he was normally stationed aboard the *Benjamin Franklin*. Unfortunately the *Franklin* was currently headed toward the Persian Gulf. Until his shoulder healed, he'd be twiddling his thumbs behind some desk and hating it.

After a while Adam felt better. His head had stopped spinning and the ache in his shoulder wasn't quite as intense. It would be easy to close his eyes and sleep but if he slept now, he'd spend the whole night staring at the ceiling.

A wife.

It was something to consider. Maybe he should resume his efforts to meet someone, with marriage in mind. The time was right. His parents wanted more grandchildren and he was certainly willing to do his part. According to Ali, he was an excellent candidate for a husband and father. She'd tried any number of times to fix him up, but nothing had ever come of her matchmaking efforts.

A wife.

He relaxed and smiled. He was ready. All he needed now was the woman.

Chapter Four

Lieutenant Commander Alison Karas had been assigned as senior medical officer aboard the *USS Woodrow Wilson*. As much as she wanted to be with Jazmine and as difficult as it had been to leave her daughter with Shana, Ali was determined to fulfill her duty to the Navy. During her twelve-year career, she'd never been stationed aboard a ship. Before Jazmine was born, she'd done everything in her limited power to get such an assignment, but it hadn't happened.

So far, she'd served in a number of military hospitals. And now, when she least wanted sea duty, that was exactly what she got. Still, she loved the Navy with the same intensity her husband had.

Her quarters were shared with another woman officer. There hadn't been time to exchange more than a brief greeting before they'd each begun their respective assignments. The crew was preparing to set out to sea. Within a couple of days, the jets would fly in from Naval air stations all over the country. It was standard procedure for the F-14s to link up with the aircraft carrier.

Unlikely though it was, she hoped for an opportunity to watch, since the pilots' precision and skill were so impressive. Pilots were a special breed, as she well knew. Peter had wanted to fly jets from the time he was in grade school, according to his mother.

She smiled sadly at the thought of her husband. The pain of his loss remained sharp and—as always—Ali hoped he hadn't suffered. There must have been a moment of sheer terror when he realized he wouldn't be able to recover. She tried not to think of that.

Trite as it sounded, she'd learned that life does go on. It hadn't seemed possible in the beginning, when she'd been blinded by her grief. She was surprised to discover that everything continued as it had before. Classes were held in Jazmine's school; the radio still played silly love songs. People drove their cars and ate meals and bickered with each other. Ali hadn't been able to understand how life as she'd once known it could go on as though nothing had changed.

Jazmine was in good hands. Shana would look after her well. Ali needed to reassure herself of that several times a day. Leaving her daughter had been traumatic, but for Jazmine's sake, Ali had tried not to let her emotions show. Before she returned to San Diego, they'd talked, and Ali had a heart-to-heart with Shana, too.

She was still a little worried about Shana, but once they'd had a chance to really discuss the situation, Ali accepted that this impulsive change in her sister's life was probably the best thing she'd done in years. Shana needed a fresh start. The ice-cream parlor was charming and would undoubtedly be a big success. Jazmine had a bit of an attitude, but that wouldn't last long. And it helped that Adam was close by. The biggest disappointment of her stay was that they hadn't been able to reach him. Once he checked his messages, she knew he'd get in touch with Jazmine.

Ali found her daughter's suggestion that she marry Adam downright amusing. Ali thought the world of her husband's best friend, but there was no romantic spark on either side. What was particularly interesting was the fact that Jazmine seemed ready to discuss bringing another man into their lives.

Despite that, Ali had no intention of remarrying. She hadn't mentioned that to either her sister or Jazmine because it sounded too melodramatic. And both of them would argue with her. But a man like Peter only came around once in a lifetime, and she wasn't pressing her luck. If, by chance, she were to consider remarrying, she was determined not to fall in love with a Navy man. She'd already had one Navy husband and she wasn't going to try for two.

Ali had never removed her wedding band. After all these years, that ring represented perhaps the most significant part of her life. And although shipboard romances were strictly prohibited, it was a form of emotional protection, too. As far as her shipmates knew, she was married and that was the impression she wanted to give.

After spending her shift in the sick bay checking supplies, Ali went to the wardroom, where the officers dined. Two other women officers were in the room but their table was full and they seemed engrossed in conversation. Sitting alone at a corner table, she felt self-conscious, although she rather enjoyed watching the men and women as they chatted. In a few weeks, she'd probably be sitting with one of those groups. Life aboard a carrier was new to her, but eventually it would become familiar and even comfortable.

Just as she was finishing her dinner, the group that included the other women was joined by Commander Dillon. Ali read his name tag as he walked past her table. He acknowledged her with a stiff nod, which she returned. From the reception he received, it was clear that he was well-liked and respected by his fellow officers. She had no idea what his duty assignment might be.

Without being obvious—at least she hoped she wasn't—she studied Dillon. He was tall and lean with dark hair graying at the temples, which led her to believe he must be in his early to midforties. His most striking feature was his intense blue eyes. To her chagrin, she found herself looking at his ring finger and noticed it was bare. Not that it meant anything. Wedding rings were dangerous aboard ship, although she chose to wear hers. More than once Ali had seen fingers severed as a result of a wedding band caught in machinery.

As soon as she'd finished her coffee, Ali went back to her work space at the clinic and logged on to the Internet to write Shana and Jazmine a short note. Her sister and daughter would be anxious to hear from her after her first full day at sea.

Sent: May 19
From: Alison.Karas@woodrowwilson.navy.mil
To: Shana@mindsprung.com
Subject: Hello!

Dear Shana and Jazmine,

Just checking in to see how things are going with you two. It's a little crazy around here and I'm still finding my sea legs. Not to worry, though.

Hey, Jazz, I was thinking you should help your aunt come up with ideas for ice-cream sundaes. Remember how we invented our own versions last summer? Hot fudge, marshmallow topping and crushed graham crackers? You called it the Give Me More Sundae. Not bad.

Shana, be sure to look over Jazz's homework, especially the math. Okay, okay, I'll stop worrying. Send me an e-mail now and then, okay? I'm waiting with bated breath to hear how you two are surviving.

Love ya.
Ali (That's Mom to you, Jazz!)

It wasn't much of a message, but Ali was tired and ready to turn in for the night. As she started back to her quarters, she met Commander Dillon in the long narrow passageway. She nodded and stepped aside in order to allow him to pass.

He paused as he read her badge. "Karas?"

"Yes, sir."

"At ease." He glanced down at her left hand. "Your husband is Navy?"

"Yes, sir." She looked self-consciously at her wedding ring. "He—" She'd begun to explain that she was a widow, then stopped abruptly. Rather than make eye contact, she stared into the bulkhead.

"This is your first time aboard the *Woodrow Wilson?*" The question was casual, conversational in tone.

She nodded again. "This is my first time on any ship. I'm wondering how long it's going to take before I get used to it." She laughed as she said this, because being on an aircraft carrier was so much like being in a building. Every now and then, Ali had to remind herself that she was actually aboard a ship.

Commander Dillon's eyes narrowed slightly as he smiled. "You'll be fine."

"I know I will. Thank you, sir."

That very moment, an alarm rang for a fire drill. All sailors were to report immediately to their assigned stations. A sailor rushed past Ali and jolted her. In an effort to get out of his way, she tripped and fell hard against Commander Dillon, startling them both. The commander stumbled backward but caught himself. Instinctively he reached out and grabbed her shoulders, catching her before she lost her balance and toppled sideways. Stunned, they immediately grew still.

"I'm sorry," she mumbled, shocked at the instant physical reaction she'd experienced at his touch. It had been an innocent enough situation and meant nothing. Yet it told Ali a truth she'd forgotten. She was a woman. And, almost against her will, was attracted to a man other than Peter.

He muttered something under his breath, but she didn't hear what he said and frankly she was grateful. Without another word, they hurried in opposite directions.

Ali's face burned with mortification, but not because she'd nearly fallen into Commander Dillon. When her breasts grazed him and he'd reached out to catch her, he could have pulled her to him and kissed her and she wouldn't have made a single protest. Her face burned, and she knew she was in serious trouble. No, it was just the close proximity to all these men. At least that was what Ali told herself. It wasn't the commander; it could've been any man, but even as that thought went through her mind, she knew it was a lie. She worried that the commander might somehow know what she'd been feeling. That mortified her even more.

The scene replayed itself in her head during the fire drill and afterward, when she retired to her quarters. Once she was alone, Ali found a pen and paper. It was one thing to send Jazmine an e-mail but a letter was a tangible object that her daughter could touch and hold and keep. She knew Jazmine would find comfort in reading a note Ali had actually written.

When Ali had first started dating Peter, they'd exchanged long letters during each separation. She treasured those letters and savored them all, even more so now that he was gone.

On the night of their wedding anniversary last year, while Jazmine was at a slumber party, Ali had unearthed a stack and reread each one. She quickly surrendered to self-pity, but she had every reason in the world to feel sorry for herself, she decided, and didn't hold back. That night, spent alone in her bedroom, grieving, weeping and angry, had been an epiphany for her. It was as if something inside her—a wall of pretense and stoicism—had broken wide-open, and her pain had gushed forth. She believed it was at that point that she'd begun to heal.

Oh, she'd cried before then, but this time, on the day that would have been her twelfth wedding anniversary, she'd wept as if it was the end of the world.

By midnight she'd fallen asleep on top of the bed with Peter's letters surrounding her. Thankfully Jazmine hadn't been witness to this emotional breakdown. Her daughter had known the significance of the date, however, and had given her mother a handmade anniversary card the following afternoon. Ali would always love that sweet card. After she'd read it, they'd hugged each other for a long time. Jazmine had revealed sensitivity and compassion, and Ali realized she'd done her daughter a grave disservice.

All those months after Peter's death, Ali had tried to shield Jazmine from her own pain. She'd encouraged the child to grieve, helped her deal with the loss of her father as much as possible. Yet in protecting Jazmine, Ali hadn't allowed her daughter to see that she was suffering. She hadn't allowed Jazmine to comfort her, which would have brought comfort to Jazmine, too.

Later that same day, after dinner, Ali had shared a few of Peter's letters with Jazmine. It was the first time they'd really talked about him since his death. Before then, each seemed afraid to say more than a few words for fear of upsetting the other. Ali learned how much Jazmine needed to talk about Peter. The girl delighted in each tidbit, each detail her mother supplied. Ali answered countless questions about their first meeting, their courtship and their wedding day. Jazmine must've heard the story of their first date a dozen times and never seemed to tire of it.

Once Ali's reserve was down, not a night passed without Jazmine's asking about Peter. As a young child, her daughter had loved bedtime stories and listening to Ali read. At nine she suddenly wanted her mother to put her to bed again. It was so out of character for her gutsy, sassy daughter that it'd taken Ali a couple of nights to figure out what Jazmine really wanted, and that was to talk about her father.

In retrospect Ali recognized that those months of closeness had helped prepare Jazmine for this long separation. Ali didn't think she could have left her with Shana otherwise.

Shana. An involuntary smile flashed across her face as she leaned back in the desk chair. These next six months would either make or break her strong-willed younger sister. She'd taken on a lot all at once. Buying this restaurant on impulse was so unlike her. Shana preferred to have things planned out, down to the smallest detail. Not only that, this new venture was a real switch for her after her sales position.

If there was anything to be grateful for in Shana's sudden move to Seattle, it was the fact that Brad Moore was out of her life. Ali had only met him once, during a brief visit home, but he'd struck her as sleazy, and she hadn't been surprised to hear about his duplicity. Ali wondered how he'd managed to deceive her sister all this time, but whatever charms he possessed had worked about four and a half years longer than they should have. She supposed that, like most people, Shana had only seen what she'd wanted to see.

Before she returned to San Diego, Ali and Shana were able to spend a few hours together. Jazmine was asleep and the two sisters sat on the bed in Shana's room talking.

She'd seen how hurt Shana was by Brad's un-
faithfulness. In an effort to comfort her sister, Ali had
suggested Shana try to meet someone else as quickly as
possible.

Her sister hadn't taken kindly to the suggestion. In
fact, she hadn't been shy about sharing her feelings with
regard to the male of the species. Shana claimed she was
finished with men.

"You're overreacting," Ali had told her.

"And you're being ridiculous." Sitting with her knees
drawn, Shana shook her head. "The absolute last thing
I want to do now is get involved again. I was 'involved'
for the last five years and all I got out of that relationship, besides a lot of pain, is two crystal champagne
glasses Brad bought me. He said we'd use them at our
wedding." Not that he'd actually given her an engagement ring or set the date. "Those glasses are still in the
box. If he'd thought of it, he probably would've asked
for them back."

"You feel that way about men now, but you won't
always."

Shana frowned. "You're one to talk. I don't see you
looking for a new relationship."

"Okay, fine, neither of us is interested in men."

"Permanently," Shana insisted.

Ali had laughed then and said, "Speak for yourself."

Funny, as she reviewed that conversation, Commander
Dillon came to mind. It was unlikely that she'd see him
on a regular basis; with a crew of five thousand on this
ship, their paths wouldn't cross often. Ali wasn't entirely
sure why, but she felt that was probably a good thing.

Chapter Five

The next few days were intense for Shana. She insisted on driving Jazmine to school, and every morning she joined the long line of parents dropping off their kids at the grade school. If Jazmine appreciated her efforts to build a rapport between them, she gave no indication of it. The most animation she'd witnessed in the girl had been after Monday's lengthy telephone conversation with her uncle Adam.

Shana, her aunt, a blood relative, was simply Shana, but Adam Kennedy, family friend, was *Uncle* Adam. The *uncle* part was uttered with near-reverence.

Okay, so she was jealous. Shana admitted it. While she struggled to gain ground with her niece, Jazmine droned on about this interloper.

Tuesday afternoon, the school bus again let Jazmine off in front of the ice-cream parlor. Her niece had dragged herself into the shop, as though it demanded all her energy just to open the door. Then she'd slipped onto one of the barstools and lain her head on her folded arms.

Wednesday afternoon, Shana watched the school bus approach and the doors glide open. Sure enough, Jazmine was there, but this time she leaped off the bus and hurried toward the restaurant.

Shana stopped and stared. No, it couldn't be. But it was. Jazmine had her backpack. From the size and apparent weight of it, nothing seemed to be missing, either.

The instant Jazmine stepped inside, Shana blurted out, "You've got your backpack." It probably would've been better to keep her mouth shut and let Jazmine tell her, but she'd been too shocked.

"I know." Jazmine dumped her backpack on the floor and hopped onto the barstool with a Bugs Bunny bounce, planting her elbows on the counter. "Can I have some ice cream?"

Taken aback, Shana blinked. "Who are you and what have you done with my niece?"

"Very funny."

Shana laughed and reached for the ice-cream scoop. "Cone or dish?"

"Dish. Make it two scoops. Bubblegum and strawberry." She paused, her face momentarily serious. "Oh—and thank you."

"You're welcome." Bending over the freezer, Shana rolled the hard ice cream into a generous ball. "Well," she said when she couldn't stand it any longer. "The least you can do is tell me what happened."

"With what?" Jazmine asked, then giggled like the

nine-year-old she was. "I don't know if you noticed or not, but I was pretty upset Monday afternoon."

"Really," Shana said, playing dumb.

"Two girls cornered me in the playground. One of them distracted me, and the other ran off with my backpack."

Shana clenched her jaw, trying to hide her anger. As Jazmine's legal guardian, she wanted these girls' names and addresses. She'd personally see to it that they were marched into the principal's office and reprimanded. On second thought, their parents should be summoned to the school for a confrontation with the authorities. Perhaps it would be best to bring in the police, as well.

"How'd you get it back?" Shana had given up scooping ice cream.

Looking more than a little pleased with herself, Jazmine straightened her shoulders and grinned. "Uncle Adam told me I should talk to them."

Wasn't *that* brilliant. Had she been asked, Shana would've told Jazmine the same thing.

"He said I should tell them it was really unfortunate, but it didn't seem like we could be friends and I was hoping to get to know them." This was uttered in the softest, sweetest tones Shana had ever heard from the girl.

"They fell for it?"

Jazmine's eyes widened. "I meant it. At first I thought they were losers but they're actually pretty cool. I think they just wanted to see what I carried around with me."

Frankly Shana was curious herself.

"Once they looked inside, they were willing to give it back."

"You're not missing anything?"

Jazmine shook her head.

"Great." Muttering under her breath, Shana dipped the scoop into the blue bubblegum-flavored ice cream. The bell above the door rang, but intent on her task, Shana didn't raise her head.

"I'll have some of that myself," a male voice said.

"Uncle Adam!" Jazmine shrieked. Her niece whirled around so fast she nearly fell off the stool.

Hearing his name was all the incentive Shana needed to glance up. She did just in time to watch Jazmine throw her arms around a man dressed casually in slacks and a shirt. From the top of his military haircut to the bottom of his feet, this man was Navy, with or without his uniform. His arm was in a sling and he grimaced when Jazmine grabbed hold of him but didn't discourage her hug. From the near-hysterical happiness the girl displayed, a passing stranger might think Shana had been holding Jazmine hostage.

"You must be Ali's sister," he said, smiling broadly at Shana.

She forced a smile in return. She'd been prepared to dislike him on sight. In fact, she'd never even met him and was already jealous of the relationship he had with Jazmine. Now he was standing right in front of her—and she found her tongue stuck to the roof of her mouth. He seemed to be waiting for her to reply.

"Yes, hi," she said and dropped the metal scoop into the water container, sloshing liquid over the edges. Wiping her wet hand on her white apron, she managed another slight smile. "Yes, I'm Ali's sister."

On closer inspection, she saw that he was tall and apparently very fit. Some might find his looks appealing, but Shana decided she didn't. Brad was just as tall and equally fit—from spending hours in a gym every week, no doubt admiring himself in all the mirrors. Adam's hair was a deep chestnut shade, similar to her own. No. Not chestnut, she decided next, nothing that distinguished. His was plain brown. He might've been considered handsome if not for those small, beady eyes. Well, they weren't exactly *small,* more average, she supposed, trying to be as objective as she could. He hugged Jazmine and looked at Shana and—no.

But he did. He looked at Shana and *winked.* The man had the audacity to flirt with her. It was outrageous. This was the very man Jazmine wanted her mother to marry. The man whose praises she'd sung for two full days until Shana thought she'd scream if she heard his name one more time.

"I'm Adam Kennedy." He extended his free right hand.

She offered her left hand because it was dry and nodded politely. "You mean *Uncle* Adam." She hoped he caught the sarcastic inflection in her voice.

He grinned as if he knew how much that irritated her. Okay, now she had to admit it. When he smiled he wasn't ordinary-looking at all. In fact, some women— not her, but others who were less jaded—might even be attracted to him. That she could even entertain the remote possibility of finding a man attractive was upsetting. Wasn't it only a few days ago that she'd declared to her sister that she was completely and utterly off men? And now here she was, feeling all shaky inside and acting like a girl closer to Jazmine's age than her own. This was pathetic.

In an attempt to cover her reaction, Shana handed Jazmine the bowl of ice cream with its two heaping scoops.

"Uncle Adam wants one, too," Jazmine said excitedly, and then turned to him. "What happened to your arm?" she asked, her eyes wide with concern. "Did you break it?"

"Nothing as dramatic as that," he said, elevating the arm, which was tucked protectively in a sling. "I had a problem with my shoulder, but that's been taken care of now."

Jazmine didn't seem convinced. "You're going to be all right, aren't you?"

"I'll be fine before you know it."

"Good," Jazmine said; she seemed reassured now. Taking Adam by the hand, she led him across the restaurant to a booth.

Shana could hear Jazmine whispering up a storm, but hard as she strained, she couldn't hear what was being said. Working as fast as her arm muscles would allow, she hurriedly dished up a second bowl of ice cream. When she'd bought this business, no one had mentioned how hard ice cream could be. She was developing some impressive biceps.

She smiled as she carried the second dish over to their booth and hoped he enjoyed the bright teal-blue bubblegum ice cream. After she'd set it down in front of him, she waited. She wasn't sure why she was lingering.

Jazmine beamed with joy. Seeing her niece this happy about anything made Shana feel a pang of regret. Doing her best to swallow her pride, she continued to stand there, unable to think of a thing to say.

Her niece glanced up as if noticing her for the first time. "I was telling Uncle Adam about my backpack. He's the one who said those other girls just wanted to be friends. I didn't believe him, but he was right."

"Yes, he was." Shana might have been able to fade into the background then if Adam hadn't chosen that moment to turn and smile at her. Ignoring him would be easy if only he'd stop smiling, dammit.

"The girls gave it back?" Adam's gaze returned to Jazmine.

Her niece nodded. "Madison asked me to sit next to her at lunch today and I did."

Adam reached across the table and the two exchanged a high five. "That's great!"

"Can I get you anything else?" Shana asked, feeling like a third wheel. These two apparently had a lot to discuss, and no one needed to tell her she was in the way. Besides, she had a business to run. Several customers had come in; at the moment they were studying the list of ice-cream flavors but she'd have to attend to them soon.

"Nothing, thanks." He dipped his plastic spoon into the ice cream. Then, without giving her any warning, he looked at Shana again and their eyes met. Shana felt the breath freeze in her lungs. He seemed to really *see* her, and something about her seemed to catch him unawares. His brow wrinkled as though he was sure he knew her from somewhere else, but couldn't place her.

"How long can you stay?" her niece asked.

Adam turned his attention back to Jazmine.

Shana waited, curious to know the answer herself.

"Just a couple of hours."

"Two hours!" Jazmine didn't bother to hide her disappointment.

"I've got to get back to base for a meeting."

"Right," Shana said, diving into the conversation. "He has to go back to Everett. We wouldn't want to detain him, now would we?" She didn't mean to sound so pleased about sending him on his way, but she wanted him out of there. Shana disliked how he made her feel—as if…as if she was on the brink of some important personal discovery. Like she'd told her sister, she was off men. For good. Okay, for a year. It would take that long to get Brad out of her system, she figured. Now, all of a sudden, there was this man, this uncle Adam, whose smiles made her feel hot, then cold. That wasn't a good sensation for her to be having. It contradicted everything she'd been saying—and it made her uncomfortable.

"I'll stop by again soon," Adam promised, looking directly at her as he said it.

"I want to know what happened to your arm," Jazmine insisted.

"Surgery."

"Does Mom know?"

Adam shook his head. "She's got enough on her plate without worrying about me."

"You've talked to her?" Shana demanded. She forgot that she was pretending not to listen to their conversation. Catherine, the woman who worked part-time, arrived then and immediately began taking orders while Shana handled the cash register.

Adam shifted toward her. "She e-mailed me."

"Oh." Embarrassed, Shana glanced away. "Of course."

"I wish the base were closer," Jazmine muttered.

"Everett isn't that far and with light duty, I'll have more time to spend with you."

"Exactly how soon do you have to leave this afternoon?" Jazmine pressed. "Couldn't you please, please have your meeting tomorrow?"

This kid wasn't easily put off, Shana thought. While she was more than ready to usher Adam Kennedy out the door, her niece was practically begging him to stay.

"It's not really up to me. I've got to go soon, but I'll visit as often as I can."

"He's busy, I'm sure," Shana said before his words sank into her consciousness. *He'd be back...often.* In other words, she'd better get used to having him around, and judging by that smirk, he intended to smile at her some more. Oh, great.

"As often as you can?" Jazz repeated. "What does that mean?"

"I'll make sure I'm here at least once a week to check up on my favorite girl."

Instead of shouting with happiness, Jazmine hung her head. "*Only* once a week?"

Once a week? That often? Shana's reaction was just the opposite. As far as she was concerned, weekly visits were far too frequent.

Ali's little sister seemed oversensitive, Adam observed with some amusement as Shana returned to the ice-cream counter. That wasn't the only thing he'd noticed, either. She was beautiful with classic features, dark hair and eyes and a face he found utterly appealing. Ali was a beautiful woman, too, but in a completely different way. Although both had dark brown hair and eyes, the resemblance stopped there. Shana was the taller of the two and model-thin, whereas Ali had more flesh on her. If he were ever to say that out loud, she'd no doubt be insulted, but it was the truth. Ali wasn't overweight by any means, just rounded in all the right places. In his opinion, the little sister could stand to gain a few pounds. He wasn't sure why he was concentrating on the physical, because his reaction to Shana was much more complex than that. He was attracted to her. Period. He liked what he saw and he liked what he didn't see—what he sensed about her. Attraction was indefinable, more about the sum of a person than his or her parts. People called it chemistry, sparks, magic, all sorts of vague things. But whatever you called it, the attraction was obviously there.

Something else was obvious. *She* felt it, too. And she didn't want to. In fact, she seemed determined to make sure he knew that. He didn't go around ravishing young women, willing or unwilling, but he definitely got a kick out of her reaction to him. He couldn't keep from grinning as he headed into the heavy freeway traffic on I-5 North.

On second thought, *he* might be overreacting. Perhaps it was all those musings about his lack of female companionship following his release from the hospital. Pain could do that to a man. Maybe he was wrong about Shana's interest in him; maybe he'd simply been projecting his own attraction and— Damn, this was getting much too complicated.

That same evening, when Adam logged on to the Internet, he discovered two messages from Ali. In the first, she was eager to know if he'd made contact with Jazmine; in the other, she asked if he'd be able to give her sister a break now and then. He immediately e-mailed back that he'd seen Jazz and everything seemed to be fine with her and Shana. He also said he'd visit as often as he could. Several questions regarding Shana went through his mind, but he didn't ask them, not wanting Ali to get the wrong impression. He also feared she'd relay his interest to her sister—and he just wasn't ready for that.

An hour later, his phone rang. It was Jazmine, who spoke in a whisper.

"Where are you?" he asked.

"In the closet." She was still whispering.

"What's the problem?" So Jazmine wanted to talk to him without her aunt listening in. Interesting.

"I hate it here and—oh, Uncle Adam, it's just so good to see someone I know."

Adam wished he could be there to wrap his arm around the girl's thin shoulders. "It'll get better." He didn't mean to sound trite, but he couldn't come up with anything else to say. "Didn't you tell me you'd made friends with those two girls who took your backpack?"

"Yeah, I guess, but it isn't like California. Seattle isn't like anyplace I've been. I miss my mom and…I just don't like it here."

"I feel that way whenever I've got a new duty assignment," he said, wanting to comfort her and not knowing how. "I'm in a new work environment myself and to be honest I'd much rather be in Hawaii. It's the perfect duty station. But you do get used to wherever you are, Jazz…."

"I just want to be with my mom," Jazmine said, sounding small and sad. "I wouldn't care where it was."

"Are you getting along with your aunt?"

Jazmine hesitated. "She tries, and I appreciate everything she does, I really do, but she doesn't know that much about kids." As if she felt bad about criticizing her aunt, the girl added, "It's not as bad as it was on Monday, but…"

Adam wanted to continue asking questions about Shana, but he preferred not to be obvious about it. "She seems nice."

"She is, but she's got issues, you know."

It was difficult for Adam not to laugh outright at Jazmine's solemn tone. "What kind of issues?" he asked gravely.

Jazmine snickered. "Where would you like me to start? She has this old boyfriend that she dumped or he dumped her—I don't know which—but she won't even say his name. I heard her talking to Mom, and every time she got close to mentioning his name, she called him that-man-I-used-to-date. Is that ridiculous or what?"

Adam murmured a noncommittal reply.

"That's not all. Shana used to have a regular job, a really good one for a drug company. Mom said she made fabulous money, but she quit after she broke up with this guy. Then she bought the ice-cream parlor. She doesn't know a thing about ice cream or pizza or anything else."

Still, Adam had to admire her entrepreneurial spirit. "She seems to be doing all right."

"That's only because she phones the former owners ten times a day, and I'm not exaggerating. She finally figured out she can't do everything on her own and she hired a lady to come in during the afternoons to help her. I'm only nine-going-on-ten, and *I* figured that out before she did." Jazmine stopped abruptly, as if something had just occurred to her. "You're not *attracted* to her or anything, are you?"

Adam relaxed in his chair and crossed his ankles. "Well…I think she's kinda cute."

"No, no, no!" Jazmine said, more loudly this time. "I was afraid this would happen. This is terrible!"

Adam loved the theatrics. "What is?"

"Shana," Jazmine cried as if it should all be perfectly logical. "What about *Mom?* If you're going to fall in love with anyone, make it my mom. She needs you, and you'd be a great stepdad."

"Jazmine," he said, the amusement suddenly gone. "I think the world of your mother. She's a wonderful woman, and I love her dearly, but—"

He had no idea how to put this without upsetting her. "Your mother and I, well…"

"You love her like a sister," Jazmine finished for him. She sounded resigned and not particularly surprised.

Adam almost wished he *could* fall in love with Ali. Perhaps if he'd met her before Peter did, things would've been different. But he hadn't, and now it was impossible to think of Ali in any other way.

"That's pretty astute of you," he said.

"What's astute?"

"Smart."

Jazmine sighed heavily. "Not really. I said something about you to Mom, and what she said is she loves you like a brother."

So it was a mutual feeling, which was a relief. "Did your mother tell you she was ready for another relationship?" he asked.

"I think she is," Jazmine replied after a thoughtful moment. "But I don't know if *she* knows it." She hesitated, and he could almost see her frown of concentration. "Mom's been different the last few months." She seemed to be analyzing the situation as she spoke. "She's less sad," Jazmine went on. "We talk about Dad a lot, and Mom laughs now and she's willing to do things and go places again. I guess someone mentioned that to the Navy, because they decided to give her sea duty."

"I'm grateful your mother's feeling better about life. When the time's right, she'll meet someone special enough to be your stepdad."

"But it won't be you."

Adam heard the sadness in her voice and regretted it. "It won't be me," he said quietly.

"You *are* attracted to Shana though, right?"

"Maybe." That was all he'd admit. He found himself wondering about the man Shana had recently dumped or been dumped by.

"So this guy she used to go out with—"

"They were *engaged,* I think, but she won't talk about it." There was a pause. "She didn't get a ring, though."

Engaged? Even an unofficial engagement suggested this had been a serious and probably long-term relationship. Which could explain why Shana had seemed so skittish.

"Are you gonna ask her out, Uncle Adam?"

Adam wasn't prepared to make that much of a commitment, not yet, anyway. "Uh, we'll see."

"I think she'd say yes," Jazmine said brightly. "Don't you?"

"I don't know. Some women seem to need a man in their lives, but…" His voice trailed off; he wasn't sure how to complete that thought.

Jazmine muttered a comment he couldn't hear.

"Pardon?" he said.

"Just remember, she's got issues—lots and lots of issues."

Adam managed to stifle a chuckle. "I'll do my best to keep that in mind. Listen, Jazz, do you feel okay now?"

"Yeah… I guess I should come out before Shana finds me in here. Oh!"

That small cry was followed by some muffled words, but he caught the drift of what was happening. Shana had just discovered where Jazmine had taken the phone.

Chapter Six

"You don't like him, do you?" Jazmine asked the
next day as they drove home from the restaurant. She
sat next to Shana with her arms defiantly crossed.

Shana knew better than to pretend she didn't understand that her niece was referring to Lieutenant Commander Adam Kennedy. "I think your uncle Adam
is…nice." The word was lame and the hesitation was
long, which gave Jazmine cause to look at Shana intently. But really, what else could she say? Her unexpected attraction to this man had completely
overwhelmed her. She could only hope it passed
quickly. How could she be devastated by her breakup
with Brad and at the same time, experience all the symp-
toms of extreme attraction toward another man? A man
she'd met for about five minutes and been determined
to dislike on sight.

"He's really cute, too." Jazmine seemed to feel obliged to remind her of this.

As if Shana needed a reminder.

"He is, isn't he?" Jazmine challenged.

"All right, he's cute." The words nearly stuck in her throat, but with no small effort, Shana managed to get them out. She didn't know why Jazmine was so insistent. The girl seemed to think she had a point to prove, and she wasn't letting up until she got Shana to confess she was interested in Adam Kennedy. She wasn't, of course. Okay, she was, but that was as far as it went. In other words, if he asked her out, which he wouldn't, she'd refuse. Well, she might consider it briefly, but the answer would still be no.

Jazmine was suspiciously quiet for several minutes and then gave a soft laugh. "I bet you're hot on him."

"What?" Shana nearly swallowed her tongue. The last thing she needed was Jazmine telling Adam this. "No way," she denied vehemently. She could only pray that wasn't what Jazz had said to Adam in the closet.

One glance told her Jazmine didn't buy her denial. She shouldn't have bothered to lie.

"You're saying that because of your old boyfriend, aren't you?"

"Absolutely not," Shana protested. She stepped hard on the brake at a stop sign she'd almost missed, jerking them both forward. Thank goodness for seat belts. Glaring at her niece, she asked, "Who told you that?"

Jazmine blinked wide eyes at Shana. "I overheard my mom talking to you. I wasn't listening in on your conversation, either, if that's what you're thinking. I tried to find out from Mom, but all she'd tell me was that your heart was broken, and that's why you moved to Seattle."

Shana was too tired to argue and too emotionally drained to be upset with her sister. If Ali had told Jazmine about Brad, then it was because she felt Jazmine needed to know. "I'm completely over Brad. I'm so over him it's hard to remember why I even got involved with him." The words had begun to sound like a worn-out litany.

"Brad," Jazmine said, and seemed satisfied now that she knew his name.

Shana struggled to hide her reaction. Even the mention of Brad's name irritated her. She might have worked the last twelve hours straight, and on her feet at that, but she had enough energy left to maintain her outrage toward Brad. Still, she would've preferred never to talk about him—or hear about him—ever again.

"You still have a heart, though," Jazmine pressed. "Right?"

"Of course I have a heart." Shana didn't know where this was leading and she didn't care, as long as it didn't end up on the subject of Adam Kennedy.

"That's why you're so hot on my uncle Adam." Darn.

"I am *not* hot on your *uncle* Adam."

"Are too."

"Am not."

"Are too."

"Jazmine!"

Her niece laughed and despite her irritation, Shana smiled. This was not a conversation she wanted to have, but she'd walked right into it and was determined to extricate herself as gracefully as possible. "Don't get me wrong," she said in conciliatory tones. "I think he's a very nice man, but I don't want to get involved with anyone at the moment. Understand?"

Jazmine bit her lower lip, as if she wanted to argue, but apparently changed her mind. "For how long?"

Shana decided to nip this question in the bud. "Forever."

"That long?" Jazmine threw her a crushed look. "You don't want children? That means I'll never have cousins!"

"Okay, months and months, then." At this point Shana was ready to agree to just about anything.

"Months," Jazmine repeated. She seemed to accept that—or at any rate ventured no further argument.

Shana parked in front of her house, grateful to be home. "You know what? I don't want to cook. Do you have any suggestions?"

"I can open a can of chili," Jazmine said. "I'm not very hungry."

Shana wasn't all that hungry, either. "Sounds like a perfectly good dinner to me."

"Let me do it, okay?"

"Thanks, Jazz." Shana had no intention of turning down this generous offer. "Fabulous." Then considering her role as guardian, she felt obliged to ask, "Do you have any homework?"

"A little."

Now came the dilemma. A really good substitute mother would tell Jazmine to forget dinner; Shana would rustle up a decent meal while the kid did her schoolwork. A woman of character would insist on opening that can of chili herself. But not one with tired feet and the start of a throbbing headache, brought on by all this talk about Adam Kennedy.

Once inside the house, Shana left the front door open to create a cooling breeze. She lay back on the sofa and elevated her feet. It was little wonder the Olsens had been ready to sell their restaurant. This was hard work. For part of each day, Shana had her face buried in three-gallon containers of ice cream. Her nose felt like she was suffering from permanent frostbite.

Jazmine immediately went into the kitchen and started shuffling pans, clanking one against the other. "Do you need any help?" Shana felt she had to ask, but the question was halfhearted, to say the least.

"No, thanks."

"This is really very sweet of you."

Jazmine grumbled a reply and Shana realized she'd failed again. A kid like Jazmine, who wore ankle-high tennis shoes to school, didn't take kindly to the word *sweet*. Sooner or later, Shana would need to develop a more appropriate vocabulary. Later, she decided.

A good ten minutes passed and if not for the sounds coming from the kitchen, Shana would be napping by now. Her head rested against the cushion, her feet were propped up and all was well. For the first time since she'd arrived, Jazmine was talking freely with her. She wasn't sure whether she should credit Adam Kennedy with this improvement or not. She'd rather think she was making strides in her relationship with her niece due to her own efforts.

"Uncle Adam says you need a man in your life."

Her peace shattered, and Shana's eyes sprang open. She sat up, swung around and dropped her feet to the floor. "*What* did you just say?"

Jazmine appeared in the doorway between the kitchen and the living room, wearing a chagrined expression. "I...Uncle Adam said you're the kind of woman who needs a man in her life."

That did it. She'd utterly humiliated herself in front

of him, and he thought…he *assumed* she was making some kind of play for him. This was the worst possible scenario.

"Shana?" Jazmine whispered. "You look mad."

She wondered if the smoke coming out of her ears was any indication. "That's ludicrous!"

"I'm pretty sure he meant it as a compliment."

Shana doubted it, but gave her niece credit for some fast backtracking.

"He thinks you're beautiful."

He did? Although it shouldn't have mattered, his comment gave Shana pause. "He said that?"

Jazmine hesitated. "Well, not exactly."

Okay, then. "Listen, it's not a good idea for us to talk about your uncle Adam right now." When she saw him next, she'd have plenty to say, though.

"You don't want to talk about him?"

"Nope." The kid was catching on fast.

"You don't want to talk about Brad, either."

Right again. "You could say men aren't my favorite topic at the moment."

"I guess not," Jazmine said pensively. "I won't mention either of them if that's what you want."

"I want." Her serenity gone, Shana gave up the idea of resting and joined Jazmine in the kitchen. Her niece's backpack was propped against the kitchen chair; she seemed to keep it close at all times.

Despite her intentions to the contrary, Shana gave the sexy lieutenant commander plenty of thought. What she had to do was keep her distance. She would be polite and accommodating if he wanted to spend time with Jazmine, but other than that, she'd be cool and remote. Never again would she allow him the opportunity to suggest that she needed a man—least of all him.

Jazmine stirred the chili with her back to Shana. "I probably shouldn't have said anything."

"Don't worry about it." Shana was eager to drop the subject.

"You're not mad, are you?"

"Not anymore," Shana assured her.

"You look mad."

"I'm not," she said.

"Are too."

"Am not."

"Are too."

"Am not."

They both broke out laughing. Obviously Jazz remembered that this childish interchange had amused her earlier, and she wasn't above repeating it.

Shana had to admit it felt good to laugh with her niece; it was almost like having her sister there. Jazmine was a petite version of Ali and after she'd lowered her guard, they got along well.

Shana wondered if she should clarify her position in case Adam asked Jazmine about her again or made some other ridiculous statement. No, she decided. She'd enlighten him herself.

"You know you're not getting any younger," Jazmine said out of the blue.

Once Shana got over her shock, she had to acknowledge that the kid was ruthless in achieving her goals. She went directly for the jugular. But Shana kept her response light. "After a day like this one, that's certainly true."

On Saturday morning, Jazmine agreed to come down

to the ice-cream parlor with her. In fact, Shana had no choice but to bring her. Catherine, her employee, wouldn't be in until that afternoon.

At this point Catherine was only part-time, but with the summer traffic, business was picking up and she'd need a second part-time employee. As the season progressed and the parlor was open later in the evening, she'd add more staff. The Olsens had told her that her biggest expense would be the staff payroll and warned her not to hire more people than she needed. Shana had taken their words to heart, doing as much as she could herself.

"Can I bring my Rollerblades?" Jazmine asked, standing in the doorway of her bedroom.

"Sure." Shana hated the thought of Jazmine hanging around the restaurant all day with nothing to do. Since Lincoln Park was directly across the street, there'd be plenty of paved sidewalks for her to skate. It would be a good opportunity to meet other girls her age, too.

By noon the parlor was crowded. Shana worked the pizza side and Catherine, a grandmotherly woman in her early sixties, dealt with the ice-cream orders. Catherine had been recommended by the Olsens and was great with kids. Shana had already learned a lot from her.

A young red-haired man with two children about three and five came in and ordered a vegetarian pizza and sodas. While Shana assembled the pizza, she watched the man with his kids, admiring the way he entertained them with inventive games.

Jazmine rolled into the parlor, stopped to take off her skates and before long was deep in conversation with the father and his two kids. Shana couldn't hear what was being said, but she saw the man glance in her direction and nod.

A couple of minutes later, Jazmine joined Shana in the kitchen, which was open to the main part of the restaurant.

"Hi," Shana said, sliding the hot pizza from the oven onto the metal pan. As she sliced it, the scent of the tomato sauce and cheese and oregano wafted toward her.

"He's single."

"Who?" Shana asked distractedly as she set the pizza on the counter. "Do you want to take this out to the guy with the kids?" she asked.

"Can I?" Jazmine beamed at being asked to help out.

Her niece carefully carried the pizza to the table and brought extra napkins. She chatted with the man and his children for a few more minutes, then hurried back to Shana, who was busy preparing additional pizzas. "He asked me to introduce you."

"What?"

Jazmine's eyes widened with impatience. "I was telling you earlier. He's divorced and he wants to meet you."

"Who? The guy over there with the kids?"

"Do you see any other guy in here?"

The restaurant had any number of patrons at the moment, but the young father was the only man—and the only customer looking in her direction. He saluted her with a pizza slice.

Flustered, Shana whirled around and glared at Jazmine. "Exactly what did you say to him?"

"Me? I didn't say anything—well, I did mention that you broke up with Brad, but that was only because he asked. He said he's been in here before."

Shana didn't remember him.

"I told him that my uncle Adam said you're the kind of woman who needs a man in your life."

Shana's heart stopped. "You didn't!"

"No." Jazmine hooted with laughter. "But I thought it would get a rise out of you."

The kid seemed to think she was being funny, but Shana wasn't laughing.

"Are you interested? Because if you are, let's go say hello to him. If you're not, it's no big deal."

Shana needed to think about this. "Promise me you didn't tell him I'm single."

"I did, and I said you were looking for a husband," Jazmine said gleefully. "You don't mind, do you?"

Shana felt the blood drain out of her face. Slowly turning her head, she saw the father still watching her. She jerked around again and noticed that Jazmine was grinning from ear to ear.

"Gotcha," she said and doubled over laughing.

Shana was glad someone found her embarrassment amusing.

Chapter Seven

Jazmine had her nose pressed against the living room window early on Sunday afternoon, waiting for her *uncle* Adam. He'd phoned the previous Monday, promising to take her out for the day. He'd mentioned the Museum of Glass in Tacoma, where there was a large Dale Chihuly exhibit.

Shana was almost as eager to see the lieutenant commander as her niece was, but for distinctly different reasons. She had a thing or two she wanted to say; he didn't know it yet, but the lieutenant commander was about to get an earful. How *dare* he suggest she needed a man! Every time she thought about it, her irritation grew—until she realized she couldn't keep quiet for even one more day.

At twelve-forty-seven precisely, Jazmine dashed away from the window and announced, "He's here!"

"Good." Shana resisted the urge to race outside and

confront him then and there. She'd need to bide her time. She'd waited this long—ten whole days. What was another five minutes?

Jazmine held the screen door open, swinging it wide in welcome. "You aren't late or *anything*," she boasted so eagerly it was endearing.

"Hiya, kiddo," Adam greeted Jazmine and gave her a big hug. "It's good to see you."

"You, too! It didn't seem like Sunday would ever get here."

Shana stepped forward, saying, "Hello, Adam," in cool, level tones.

He grinned boyishly and for an instant Shana faltered. But no, she wasn't about to let him dazzle her with one of his smiles. Not this time. Her defenses were up. As far as she was concerned, he had some serious explaining to do. Still, she had to admit this guy was gorgeous. Well, *gorgeous* might be a slight exaggeration, but with those broad shoulders and the way his T-shirt fit snugly across his chest, she couldn't very well ignore the obvious. His arm was out of the sling now.

"You'd better grab a sweater," Shana suggested and Jazmine instantly flew out of the room, eager to comply so they could leave.

This was the minute Shana had been waiting for. "It's time you and I had a little talk," she said, crossing her arms.

"Sure," he said with another of those easy grins.

Again she faltered, nearly swayed by his smile, but the effect didn't last. "I want you to know I didn't appreciate the comment you made about me being—and I quote—'the kind of woman who needs a man.'"

To his credit, his gaze didn't waver. "Jazmine told you that, did she?"

So it was true. "As a matter of fact, Jazmine has re-peated it any number of times."

"I see." He glanced toward the bedroom door; Jaz-mine hadn't come out yet.

Shana sincerely hoped she'd embarrassed him. He deserved it. "I don't know where you get off making comments like that but I have a few things to say to you."

"Go right ahead." He gestured as though granting her permission to speak. That must be how it was in the mil-itary, she thought. These officers seemed to think they could say and do whatever they pleased—*and* they got to boss other people around. Well, Shana wasn't mili-tary and she felt no restraint in speaking her mind. And she refused to call this guy by his title. He wasn't *her* commander.

"Are you married, *Mr.* Kennedy?" She already knew the answer and didn't give him an opportunity to re-spond. "I believe not. Does being single make you feel in any way incomplete?" Again he wasn't allowed to an-swer. "I thought not. This might come as a shock to you, but I am perfectly content with my life as it is. In other words, I don't need a man and your insinuating that I do is an insult."

"Shana—"

"I'm not finished yet." She held up her hand, cutting him off because she was just getting started. Before he left, she expected a full apology from Adam Kennedy.

"By all means continue," he said, his pose relaxed.

His attitude annoyed her. He acted as though he was indulging her, which Shana found condescending. "Since you're single you must want a woman in your life." She gave him the once-over. "In fact, you look like a man who *needs* a woman."

To her horror, Adam simply laughed.

"I was trying to make a point here," Shana said in as dignified a tone as she could manage.

"I know," he said and made an attempt to stifle his humor.

That only served to irritate her further. "Never mind. I can see my opinion is of little interest to you."

Suddenly they both turned to see Jazmine, who stood rooted in the bedroom doorway, a sweatshirt draped over her arm. "I should've kept my mouth shut, right?" she murmured apologetically. "I'm afraid Aunt Shana might've taken what you said the wrong way."

"So I gathered." He looked down, but Shana saw that the corners of his mouth quivered.

"Shana's right, you know," Jazmine stated for Adam's benefit, as she moved toward them. "You do need someone special in your life."

Adam's smile disappeared.

Aha! She wondered how he'd feel being on the other side.

"Jazmine took your comments to heart," Shana primly informed him. "She tried to match me up with a divorced father of two."

Adam's gaze shot to Jazmine.

"Well… It didn't work out—but I'd be a good matchmaker."

As far as Shana could tell, Jazmine was completely serious. *That* had to stop. She certainly didn't need her niece dragging eligible bachelors into the pizza kitchen every chance she got.

"He might've been interested, too," Jazmine added. "He seemed really nice."

"I don't need anyone's help, thank you very much," Shana insisted.

"Hold on," Adam said, glancing from one to the other. He motioned at Jazmine. "Go back to the beginning because I think I missed something."

"I found out he was single and I told him my aunt was, too, but that was all I did. She wouldn't let me introduce her."

"This is entirely your fault." Shana felt it was important that Adam understand it was his comment that had begun this whole awkward situation.

"You're finished with Brad," Jazmine reminded her. She turned to Adam and added, "He's the guy previously known as the-man-I-used-to-date. Sort of like Prince. That's what Mom said, anyway."

Adam burst out laughing.

"There is a point to this, isn't there?" Shana asked her niece.

Jazmine nodded and threw one fist in the air. "Get out there, Aunt Shana! Live a little."

Adam laughed even more.

"You think this is funny, don't you?" Shana muttered. He wouldn't find it nearly as funny when Jazmine was busy selling his attractions to single women in the museum.

"I'm sorry." But he didn't look it. For her niece's sake, she resisted rolling her eyes.

"I think it's time we cleared up this misunderstanding," he said and gestured toward the sofa. "Why don't we all sit down for a moment?"

Shana didn't take a seat until Adam and Jazmine had already made themselves comfortable on the sofa.

To her chagrin, Adam smiled patiently as if explaining the situation to a child. "I'm afraid Jazmine read more into my comment than I intended," he began. "What I said was that *some* women seem to need a man in their lives. I wasn't talking about you. Although, of course, any man in his right mind would be attracted to you. You're a beautiful woman."

"Oh." It would be convenient if Shana could magically disappear about now, but that was not to be. "I see. Well, in that case, I won't hold you up any longer." She sprang to her feet, eager to get them both out the door before she dissolved into a puddle at his feet. "I—that's a very nice thing to say…" She stared at her watch.

Adam took the hint and stood, and Jazmine rose with him. "Is there any special time you want her back this evening?" he asked.

"No…anytime is fine," she said, then quickly reconsidered. "On second thought, Jazmine has school tomorrow so she shouldn't be out too late."

"I'll have her here by seven."

"Thank you." Shana waited by the door as they left, her heart going a little crazy as she tried to regain her composure.

"Bye, Aunt Shana."

"Bye."

She closed the door. She'd hoped to put the mighty naval officer in his place and all she'd managed to do was amuse him. Depressed, Shana sank into the closest chair and hid her face in her hands—until she realized something. For the first time since Jazmine had arrived, she'd called her Aunt Shana. Twice.

Apparently her status had been sufficiently elevated that the nine-year-old was no longer ashamed to be related to her. That, at least, was progress.

* * *

Adam waited until they'd almost reached Tacoma before he mentioned the scene at Shana's. Jazmine had barely said a word from the moment they'd left. Now and then she glanced in his direction, as if she was afraid he was upset, but really he had no one to blame but himself. He did know women who were lost without a relationship, although he didn't think Shana was like that. Intentionally or not, Jazz had misunderstood his remark and used it for her own purposes.

"You really did it this time," he murmured.

"Are you mad?"

"No, but your aunt was."

"I know, but don't you be mad, okay?"

"I shouldn't have said anything. You and I should not have been discussing male-female relationships."

"Did you mean what you said about my aunt being beautiful and all that?"

"Yes." This was only the second time he'd seen Shana; again, he'd come away wanting to know her better. He might have ruined any chance of that, but he hoped not. When he'd started out from Everett, he'd considered inviting Shana to join them. But it hadn't taken him long to decide that today probably wasn't opportune.

"What I told your aunt is the truth. She is a beautiful woman," he said casually as he headed south on the interstate.

"She likes you."

Adam chuckled.

"No, I'm serious. She's got the hots for you. I can tell."

"I don't think so." Back to reality. Shana might be attracted to him, but she'd never admit that now.

"I know so!"

"Jazmine, listen…"

"Okay, but can I say what I want to first?"

Apparently she was taking lessons from her aunt Shana. "Fine."

"I was thinking about what you said—about not feeling sparks with Mom. But I thought you might with Aunt Shana."

"Jazmine, you're far too interested in matters that are none of your concern. How do you know about this stuff, anyway? MTV?"

She groaned. "Why do adults always say things like that?"

"Because they're true."

"All I want is for you to marry her and be happy."

"Uh…"

"Has the cat got your tongue?" Jazmine teased. "Adults say that, too. No, really, I *am* serious. If you married my aunt Shana, everything would be perfect. She needs a husband and you need a wife."

"I don't need a wife," he argued. "And it's none of—"

"But you'd like to be married one day, wouldn't you?" she broke in.

"Yes," he said reluctantly. He'd had the very same thought just recently, but he'd credited that to feeling sorry for himself after the surgery. Granted, Shana was attractive but he didn't need a nine-year-old playing matchmaker. Although… He smiled involuntarily. Shana appealed to him, and he was more and more inclined to pursue the relationship. On his own schedule and in his own way.

"I can help," Jazmine offered.

"It would be best if you left this between your aunt and me. Agreed?"

After a moment, Jazmine nodded. "Agreed."

"Good, now let's have a wonderful day, all right?"

Jazmine turned a smile of pure joy on him. "All right."

A surprise awaited him when they arrived at the Museum of Glass. The Dale Chihuly exhibit was in the Tacoma Art Museum and Union Station, not in the nearby Museum of Glass. Jazmine and Adam took the guided walking tour of his permanent display and were awestruck by the Bridge of Glass. The five-hundred-foot pedestrian bridge linked the Tacoma waterfront to Pacific Avenue.

Originally Adam had gotten information about Chihuly over the Internet when he was researching a destination for today's outing. Chihuly was known for his massive glass installations, but the man's talent was even more impressive than Adam had realized. Both he and Jazmine loved his vibrant use of color and unique style. Following the walking tour, they stopped at the Museum of Glass. Adam was in for a surprise there, too. The museum was huge: it contained thirteen thousand square feet of open exhibition space. Jazmine was enthralled by the Hot Shop Amphitheater, which was the building's most striking feature. Cone-shaped, it leaned at a seventeen-degree angle, and was ninety feet high and a hundred feet wide. The theater included a glass studio where a team of artists blew and cast glass. Afterward, Adam and Jazmine ate sandwiches in the museum café and visited the gift shop. When Adam had suggested this, it had seemed like an entertaining thing to do, but he'd quickly become caught up in the excitement and drama of watching the artists work.

By the end of the afternoon, he needed a break, and

sat with a cup of coffee while Jazmine leafed through a book he'd bought her.

Before they left, Jazmine bought a postcard of the Dale Chihuly glass flowers displayed on the ceiling of a Las Vegas casino to send her mother.

"Are you ready to go back to your aunt's?" he asked, sipping his coffee.

"I guess," Jazmine said. "But only if you are."

Adam recognized a trap when he saw one. If he appeared too eager, little Jazmine might suspect he wanted to see Shana again. He did, but he sure wasn't going to admit it, especially to her.

Chapter Eight

For Shana, having an entire Sunday to herself was sheer luxury. Catherine was working at the restaurant and this was the first day she'd taken off since she'd purchased the business. Shana intended to take full advantage of this gift of time.

Working as many hours as she did, she'd been putting off a number of tasks and spent two hours doing paperwork. The Olsens had trained her well in every aspect of owning a restaurant, but they'd failed to warn her how much paperwork was involved. Getting everything organized wasn't difficult but it was time-consuming. After working all day and handling the closing in the evening, she was exhausted, and making sense of anything more than the remote control was beyond her.

Once the paperwork was up-to-date, she polished her toenails, and between three loads of wash, she luxuriated in a new mystery she'd been trying to read for weeks. She'd been reading at night in fits and starts, but couldn't manage more than fifteen or twenty minutes at a time. The author was one of her favorites but to Shana's surprise her mind kept wandering away from the page. She supposed it was because she felt guilty about all the things she should be doing.

When she wasn't fretting over that, her thoughts were on Jazmine and Adam. She knew they were going to the Museum of Glass, but that couldn't possibly take all afternoon. Well, maybe it could; she didn't know.

Finally Shana gave up and shut the book. This was Adam Kennedy's fault. Even when he was nowhere in sight, he wouldn't leave her alone.

When she could stand it no longer, Shana logged on to the computer and left her sister a message.

Sent: Sunday, June 12
From: Shana@mindsprung.com
To: Alison.Karas@woodrowwilson.navy.mil
Subject: Adam Kennedy: Friend or Foe?

Dear Ali,

Just checking in to let you know that despite our rocky start, everything's going well with Jazz and me. She's a great kid.

The upcoming week is the last of the school year. I'm thrilled at how quickly Jazmine has adjusted and how fast she's made friends. I guess she's had lots of practice. She's a tremendous help at the ice-cream and pizza parlor and insists on taking pizzas to the customers' tables, which I appreciate.

The other reason I'm writing is that I've got a question about Peter's friend, Adam Kennedy. I must have met him at Peter's funeral, but if so I don't remember. Jazmine seems to think you're romantically interested in him. Are you? You've never mentioned him before—at least not that I can recall. Before you make anything of this inquiry, I want it understood that I find him arrogant and egotistical. Jazmine, however, thinks the guy walks on water. They're off this afternoon to explore some glass museum. I'd be grateful if you'd tell me what you know about him. For instance, has he ever been married? If not, why? I don't want to give you the wrong impression or anything—I *do* find him arrogant. But he sort of interests me, too. Fill in the blanks for me, would you?

Love,
Shana

At six Shana tossed a salad for dinner. The house seemed terribly quiet, and she turned on the television for company. That wasn't like her. In all her years of living alone, she'd never once felt this lonely. At first she wondered if it was due to the breakup with Brad, but all she felt when she thought about him was regret for all that wasted time—and anger. She was just plain glad he was out of her life. In fact, she rarely thought of him at all and that surprised her.

Jazmine had been with her for only a few weeks, and already Shana couldn't imagine life without her. She missed Jazmine's energy—blaring her music or talking on the phone, or plying Shana with questions about all sorts of things. The difference between the unhappy nine-year-old who'd arrived on her doorstep and the girl she was now—well, it seemed nothing short of astonishing. She'd become extroverted, interested and...interfering.

A little after seven, Jazmine burst into the house. "I'm back!" she shouted.

Before Shana could issue a word of welcome, Jazmine regaled her with details of how they'd spent their day. She talked about the walking tour and chattered excitedly about watching the artists work in the Museum of Glass. She'd fed the seagulls along the waterfront on Rustin Way and then Adam had taken her for a quick visit to the zoo at Point Defiance Park. Shana could hardly believe the girl could talk so fast and breathe at the same time.

"I guess you had a completely rotten time?" Shana asked, teasing her. Shana realized as she spoke that the lieutenant commander was nowhere in sight. "Where's Adam?"

"We were kind of late and he had to get back." Jazmine's smile widened. "Did you *want* him to come inside?"

"Not really. I just thought he might like to...visit for a few minutes." Actually, after the way she'd torn into him on his arrival, she didn't blame him for avoiding her.

"We should probably have a little talk," Shana said, slipping an arm around Jazmine's shoulders.

Her niece stiffened. "I have a feeling this is the same little talk Uncle Adam and I had, only now it's going to be the Aunt Shana version."

Her interest was instantly piqued. "Really? And what did Adam have to say?"

Jazmine gave a long-suffering sigh. "That it would be a good idea if I left the two of you alone."

"He's right." Shana was grateful Adam had taken it upon himself to explain this. Jazmine would accept it more readily coming from him.

"He also said I'm concerning myself with matters that aren't any of my business."

"Exactly." Obviously Adam had been very forthright during his version of the "little talk."

"I promised him I wouldn't try matching you up with other men."

"I'd appreciate that," Shana said solemnly.

Jazmine sighed again. "I wouldn't like it if you went around talking to boys about me."

That was exactly how Shana had planned to approach the subject herself. "Did Adam make that comparison?"

Her niece nodded. "He said it on the drive back."

"He's smarter than he looks," Shana muttered. Then, because she felt her niece should know this, she added, "A man and a woman can be friends without being romantically involved, Jazmine. It's called a platonic relationship."

The phone rang then, and without waiting for a second ring, Jazmine leaped like a gazelle into the other room. She ripped the receiver off the wall. "Hello," she said urgently. "No, she's here, you have the right number." Jazmine held out the phone. "It's for you."

Shana started to ask who it was, but didn't. Taking the receiver, she raised it to her ear. "This is Shana."

"Shana. I can't tell you how wonderful it is to hear the sound of your voice."

For the first time in her life, Shana's knees felt as if they were about to buckle. It was Brad.

"Hello, Brad," she said evenly, amazed at her ability to respond without emotion. The man had guts; she'd say that for him. "How'd you find me?" she asked coolly.

"It wasn't easy. It's taken me weeks."

She supposed she should be complimented that he'd made the effort, but she wasn't. "I don't mean to be rude, but there was a reason I kept my number unlisted."

"The least you can do is listen to what I have to say," he told her.

"Everything's been said."

"But Shana—"

"There's nothing more to say," she insisted.

"At least give me your address. I can't believe you're living in Washington. Did you get a transfer?"

"That's nothing to do with you."

Jazmine was watching her carefully, eyes wide and quizzical as if she was hoping to memorize each word so she could repeat it.

"I would prefer if you didn't phone me again." Shana was prepared to cut him off, but he stopped her, obviously guessing her intentions.

"Don't hang up," he pleaded. "Please, Shana, just hear me out."

"It won't do any good." She'd gone ramrod-straight, her resistance up. She didn't even find this difficult, although she had to admit she was mildly curious as to why he'd sought her out.

"I don't care. I need to get this off my chest. Just promise me you'll listen."

She didn't want to encourage him with a response.

He continued despite that. "You told me you were leaving Portland, but I didn't believe you. Shana, I miss you. I need you. Nothing is the same without you. I feel so empty. You have no idea how awful it's been for me."

That was their problem in a nutshell. The entire relationship had revolved around Brad Moore and his needs. *He* missed her, *he* needed her. She was convenient, loyal and endlessly patient. Well, no more.

She rolled her eyes and made a circular motion with her hand as though to hurry him along.

Jazmine planted her hand over her mouth to smother her giggles.

"Are you listening?" he asked, finishing up a five-minute soliloquy about how much he missed all their special times. Translation: all the "special" times when she'd been there to see to his comfort. He recounted the little ways she'd indulged him—the meals she'd cooked according to his likes and dislikes, the movies she'd watched because he'd chosen them, the Christmas shopping she'd done for him... Not once did he say any of the things that might have changed her mind, including the fact that he loved her.

So far, everything he'd said reaffirmed her belief that she'd made the right decision. It would always be about Brad and what he needed from her and how important she was to his comfort. Apparently Sylvia wasn't nearly as accommodating as Shana.

Finally she couldn't take it any longer.

"Are you finished yet?" she asked and yawned rudely to signal her boredom.

Her question was followed by a short silence. "You've changed, Shana."

"Yes," she told him in a curt voice. "Yes, I have."

"I can't believe you don't love me anymore."

Shana noticed he hadn't even bothered to ask about the girl who'd answered the phone.

Brad seemed shocked that she wasn't ready to race back into his arms just because he'd made an effort to find her. A short while ago, she'd been grateful for each little crumb he'd tossed her way. Those days were over. Oh, this felt good. *She* felt good.

"What's happened to my sweet Shana?" he asked. "This isn't like you."

"I woke up," she informed him, "and I didn't respect the woman I'd become. It was time to clean house. Out with the old and in with the new."

The line went silent as he absorbed this. "You're dating someone else, aren't you?"

The temptation to let him believe that was strong, and she might have given in to it, if not for Jazmine. With her niece listening to every word, Shana felt honor-bound to tell the truth.

"It's just like you to think that, but no, I'm not seeing anyone else." She bit back the words to tell him she could if she wanted to. Well, there was that single father who might've been interested—and Adam Kennedy.

His relief was instantaneous. "You'll always love me…."

"No," she said firmly. "I won't. I don't. Not anymore. For your sake and mine, please don't call me again."

He started to argue, but Shana wasn't willing to listen. She should've hung up the phone long before, but some perverse satisfaction had kept her on the line.

As she replaced the receiver, she looked over at Jazmine. Her niece gave a loud triumphant shout. "Way to go, Aunt Shana!"

They exchanged high fives. Shana felt exuberant and then guilty for not experiencing even the slightest disappointment. She was actually grateful Brad had phoned because this conversation had provided complete and final proof that she'd reclaimed her own life.

"Can I tell Uncle Adam about this?" Jazmine asked happily.

"Adam?" Her suspicions immediately rose to the surface. "Whatever for?"

"Because," Jazmine replied as if it should be obvious. "He should know that you really are over Brad. The door's open, isn't it? I mean, you're cured."

Shana liked the analogy. "I am cured, but let's just keep this between us for now, okay?"

Jazmine frowned. "If you say so," she said without enthusiasm.

The kid was certainly eager to get her and Adam together. Presumably she'd abandoned her earlier hopes for Adam and her mother. "I want your promise that you won't talk to Adam about any part of my conversation with Brad."

Muttering under her breath, Jazmine shook her head. Halfway to her room, she turned back. "Uncle Adam wanted me to tell you he'll be by next Saturday. That's all right, isn't it?"

"Of course it is." Not until later did Shana realize how dejected she was at the thought of waiting almost a week before she saw Adam Kennedy again.

Chapter Nine

Ali read Shana's e-mail a second time and smiled. This was exactly what she'd hoped—but didn't dare believe—would happen. Although her sister was skirting the issue, she was interested in Adam; her e-mail confirmed it. Adam had definitely gotten Shana's attention.

It took half an hour for Ali to answer her sister. She worked hard on the wording for fear she'd say too much or not enough. Adam was a lot like Peter in the ways that really mattered. He was loyal, compassionate, with a strong work ethic and an endearing sense of humor. Through the years, Peter had encouraged him to settle down and get married. Personally Ali didn't understand why Adam hadn't. Aside from the important stuff, he was good-looking. As far as she knew he dated, but obviously hadn't found the one woman with whom he wanted to spend the rest of his life. Could Shana be that woman? Far be it from her to suggest such a thing. Much better if a relationship developed without her meddling. From the sounds of it, they were getting all the romantic assistance they needed—or didn't need— from Jazmine.

Once she'd finished her e-mail, Ali prepared for her shift. It'd taken some adjustment, but she'd become accustomed to life aboard the aircraft carrier. Routine helped pass the days, and being able to stay in touch with her daughter through the Internet eased her mind about Jazmine.

The hours went by quickly as she responded to small medical emergencies.

She was almost finished with her shift when Commander Frank Dillon entered the sick bay. His complexion was sickly pale, and his forehead was beaded with sweat. When he saw that Ali was the duty nurse, he attempted a weak smile but she noticed that his jaw was clenched and he was clearly in pain.

Ali remembered him from her first day in the wardroom. Since then, she hadn't seen him at all but thought about him often, reliving those few seconds when he'd reached out to steady her in the passageway. Just seconds—it couldn't have been more than that. She didn't know why she'd read anything into such a minor incident. Still, she'd fantasized about him an embarrassing number of times in the weeks since. No one had to remind her of the professional issues involved in fraternization aboard ship.

"Commander Dillon," Ali said, coming forward to assist him. He held his hand pressed against his side. "What happened?"

"Something's wrong," he muttered. He looked as if he was close to passing out. "I need a doctor."

Ali led him into an examination room, and learned that he'd had a stomachache for the last couple of days. It'd had grown steadily worse and now the pain had become intolerable. She alerted Captain Robert Coleman, the physician on duty, who examined the commander.

Ali suspected it was his appendix, and apparently Dr. Coleman did, too. Following the examination, he ordered X-rays. Ali accompanied Commander Dillon while the X-rays were taken. The commander didn't utter a word, although she knew every touch, no matter how gentle, brought him pain.

One look at the film confirmed her fears. Time was critical; judging by the amount of pain he was suffering, his appendix could rupture any minute. Dr. Coleman scheduled emergency surgery, which he planned to perform immediately.

Ali helped prep the commander, explaining what was happening and why. She hooked up the IV and taped the needle in place. After checking the fluid bag, she glanced down and discovered him watching her. She smiled shyly, unaccustomed to such intent scrutiny.

Frank closed his eyes and drew in a deep breath.

Ali squeezed his hand. "Don't worry, we'll have you back to your command as good as new," she promised.

He was silent until just before he was rolled into the surgical bay. He gripped Ali's hand unexpectedly and with surprising strength. Half rising from the gurney, he said, "It's bad. Listen, if I don't make it…if there are complications…"

"You're going to live to tell about this, Commander,"

she assured him. She gave his hand another squeeze and urged him back down. Their eyes met and she did her best to let him know that the medical staff would take good care of him and all would be well.

The commander dragged in another deep breath. "I don't mean to sound fatalistic, but I don't have any family. My wife left me years ago—no kids. My brother died a few years back and I've never updated my will."

"I'm sorry about your brother," she told him softly.

His hand clutched hers. "Money to charity. Decide for me. Promise you'll decide for me."

"I will, but, Commander…"

He wasn't listening anymore, she realized. The pain was too intense.

"I'm going into surgery with you," she whispered. "If God decides it's your time, He'll have to argue with me first." Although she was certain he was past hearing anything, she thought she detected a faint smile.

As the surgery progressed, Ali wanted to chastise the commander for waiting so long to seek medical attention. He had risked his life because of—what? Pride? Ignoring the pain hadn't made it go away. An infected appendix was not going to heal itself.

The surgery was routine until they found that, exactly as she'd suspected, the appendix had burst. Extra time and care was needed to ensure that the infection was completely eradicated before it could spread to the entire abdominal area. Peritonitis could be fatal. Having a ruptured appendix wasn't as life-threatening as in years past, but it was serious enough.

After the surgery, Commander Dillon's incision was closed and he was taken into Recovery. Lieutenant Rowland was sent in to replace Ali, whose shift had ended.

"I'll stay with him a bit longer," she told Rowland. Sitting at the commander's bedside, she took his blood pressure every twenty minutes until he woke from the anesthesia several hours later.

He moved his head instinctively toward Ali, who sat by his side.

She smiled and touched his brow. "God didn't put up much of an argument. It seems that neither heaven nor hell was interested in collecting your soul, Commander."

"You sure about that?" he whispered weakly. "I thought this pain meant I was in hell."

"How are you feeling now?"

"Like someone hacked me open with a saw blade."

"I'll give you something for the pain." She stood and reached for his chart to make a notation. "Rest now. Your body's had quite a time of it." That was an understatement, but she felt better knowing he was awake. His vital signs confirmed that he was out of immediate danger.

Ali sat with the commander for another hour and then reluctantly turned her patient over to Rowland.

"Do you know the commander?" the lieutenant asked as she left the recovery area.

"I met him our first day out."

Rowland seemed surprised that she'd stayed with him. It surprised Ali, too. She was busy these days and got as little as four or five hours' sleep a night, but hadn't been able to make herself leave. One thing was certain: this man had her attention. Just as Adam had Shana's...

Frank Dillon was lost in a dark, lonely world. Every so often he heard a soft, feminine voice and it confused him. He couldn't figure out where he was. Then he remembered the pain, the surgery, the nurse—that soft voice was the nurse talking to him. The one who haunted his dreams. He prayed it was her and in the same breath pleaded for God to send her away. Her touch was light, and on the rare occasions when he found the strength to open his eyes, she was standing by his side.

She smelled good. Not of flowers or perfume, but a distinct womanly scent. Clean and subtle and…just nice. It lured him unlike anything else he'd ever experienced. He wasn't a man accustomed to the ways of women. He'd lived his life in the Navy and for the Navy, and he'd learned the hard way that he wasn't meant to be a Navy husband.

He'd married at twenty-five and Laura had left him two years later. That had been nearly twenty years ago. His wife had walked out when she realized no amount of crying, pleading or cajoling would persuade him to resign his commission. She knew before they were married that he'd made the Navy his career, the same as his father and grandfather had. Nothing was more important to Frank than duty and honor. Not his marriage, not Laura, not one damn thing. She hadn't been able to reconcile herself to that and he doubted any woman ever could. Other commitments took second place to military life. He'd accepted that, and dedicated himself to his career. Not once in all those years had he regretted his decision. Until now—and now he would willingly have sold his soul to keep this woman at his side. He needed her, wanted her and he didn't care what it cost him.

Some of his fellow officers had been against letting women serve at sea. Frank hadn't been one of them. Now he wasn't so sure his peers had been wrong. Senior Medical Officer Alison Karas had taken up far more of his thoughts than warranted. He'd decided from their first, chance encounter to stay away from her; he wasn't risking his career for a shipboard romance. Avoiding her was easy enough to accomplish with five thousand sailors aboard the *USS Woodrow Wilson.* It was just his luck that she was the one on duty. Luck or fate? He wasn't sure he'd like the answer.

A cool hand touched his brow, followed by Alison's quiet voice. Unable to make out the words, Frank thought it might have been a prayer. Apparently he was worse off than he'd known, although she seemed to think she had some influence with the Man Upstairs. Her constancy touched him. No one had ever done anything like that before—not for him.

The darkness didn't bother him anymore. He was at peace, even though a vague memory, something about Alison, hovered just out of reach. She was with him. He planned to tell her how much her presence meant to him.

If he lived through this.

The next morning, the *USS Woodrow Wilson* was hit by a raging storm. The massive ship had turned into the typhoon, and there was nothing to do but ride it out. Thankfully, Ali had never been prone to seasickness, but a number of men were sent to sick bay. She had her hands full the first day of the storm, but things had settled down by the second. During a quiet moment, she went in to check on Commander Dillon. He was sitting up in bed, still pale and not in the best of moods.

"What the hell is going on topside?" he demanded the moment he saw her.

"We're in the midst of a typhoon, Commander."

He tossed aside his sheet and seemed ready to climb out of bed. "Get me out of here."

"No." She prevented him from moving farther.

From the way his eyes widened, Ali could tell that it wasn't often anyone stood up to the high and mighty commander. "I'm the navigator and I'm needed topside," he argued, his face reddening.

"This might come as a shock, Commander Dillon, but the Navy stayed afloat without you for more than two hundred years. They'll manage to survive for another day or so. Now stay in bed, otherwise I'll have you restrained."

His blue eyes flared. "You wouldn't."

Although her heart was pounding, Ali didn't dare let her nervousness show. "I don't think that's something you'd like to find out. Your orders are to stay in bed until Captain Coleman says otherwise. Do I make myself clear?"

His gaze challenged hers, but then, apparently reaching a decision, he nodded. Although he wasn't happy about it, he would abide by what he knew was best.

Ali was grateful. Under normal circumstances, the commander wasn't a man to cross; she'd figured that out quickly enough. And if his scowl was any indication, he was on the mend. He'd been in bad shape the first few days, but his improvement was steady. To show him how much she appreciated his cooperation, she patted his arm.

He stiffened as if he found her touch offensive and Ali quickly backed away. While he was under anesthesia, she'd touched him many times. In an effort to comfort him, she'd stroked his brow and talked to him in soothing tones. She'd frequently taken his pulse and blood pressure and let her hand linger on his arm, hoping he'd sense her encouragement and concern. Perhaps she'd grown too familiar, too personal.

"I apologize," he muttered gruffly.

Embarrassed, Ali retreated an additional step. "No, the fault is mine—I'm sorry." By all rights, she should turn and leave. The clinic was busy. Sailors were waiting. She should get while the getting was good, as her grandmother used to say.

"You were with me in Recovery until I regained consciousness, weren't you?" he whispered.

She nodded, afraid they were taking a dangerous risk by acknowledging this attraction. Not since Peter's death had Ali allowed herself to feel anything for another man. In fact, she'd been certain she never would and now...now she wasn't sure what to think.

"Any particular reason you stayed with me all those hours?" he asked.

Ali didn't know what to tell him. Honesty might be the best policy, but there were times the truth was better avoided. This appeared to be one of those times.

"Your appendix had ruptured, Commander. In such cases, there's a significant chance of complications. It was easier for me just to remain on duty than explain the situation to my shift replacement." Ali used her best professional voice, making it as devoid of emotion as she could.

He seemed to accept her explanation and answered with an abrupt nod.

"Is there anything else I can do for you?" she asked, moving away from his bedside.

"Not a thing," he replied in clipped tones, and Ali knew he was referring to a whole lot more than his medical situation.

Chapter Ten

As promised, Adam Kennedy was at the restaurant by ten on Saturday morning. Shana had anticipated this moment—no, dreaded it—all week. She might've been able to push the lieutenant commander from her mind if it weren't for Jazmine, who found every excuse in the world to bring up his name. They could be discussing the migration habits of Canada geese, and Jazmine would somehow link the topic with her uncle Adam. It didn't matter *what* they discussed, Adam Kennedy became part of the conversation.

Shana didn't resent the fact that her niece called Adam her uncle anymore. It seemed natural for her to do so. What didn't seem natural—or fair—was the way he'd infiltrated her thoughts. And, in all honesty, that wasn't just due to Jazmine.

"Good morning," Adam said as he marched into the

restaurant with a crisp military gait that said he was ready for action. He wore black jeans and a casual denim shirt with the sleeves rolled up.

"Hi." Her voice faltered a little. This was one attractive man, a fact she was trying hard to ignore. Nonetheless, her hands trembled as she reached for a paper towel and wiped them clean. "Jazmine brought her Rollerblades." Thankfully it was early enough that the ice-cream parlor didn't have any customers yet.

"I saw. She put on a show for me in the parking lot."

"Oh." Now *that* was an intelligent response and Shana resisted the urge to kick herself. She intensely disliked the way Adam made her feel like an awkward teenager. Until recently, she'd considered herself a competent professional, a woman who could cope with any social situation, and it irked her no end that this man could agitate her like this. "Where are you two headed today?" she asked conversationally, hoping to hide her complete lack of a brain.

Adam sauntered up to the cash register, apparently in no hurry to leave. "I haven't decided yet. I thought I'd get some suggestions from Miss Jazz."

"Good idea." Before she sent him off with Jazmine, perhaps she should enlighten him about her niece's continuing efforts to match up the two of them. "Do you have a few minutes before you go?"

"Sure." He slid onto one of the stools.

Rubbing her palms against her apron, Shana took a moment to clear her thoughts. "I don't know if you've noticed," she began, "but Jazmine seems to be working hard at, uh, getting the two of us together." She paused. "This is in spite of your...little talk."

Adam leaned forward. "I got the hint in our last

phone conversation, when she started mentioning your name in practically every sentence."

"She does that to you, too?" Interesting. And, she supposed, predictable. "You're a frequent topic of conversation yourself."

He chuckled. "She's been e-mailing me updates on you."

"Updates on *what?*"

"I haven't paid a lot of attention."

She was unexpectedly miffed by that but decided his indifference was probably for the best.

"By the way, how's Brad?"

Shana nearly bit her tongue in an effort to hide her reaction. "I thought you said you weren't paying attention," she said. "Brad isn't important."

"Really? That's curious because—"

"I have something to discuss," she said, cutting him off before they both got sidetracked by the unpleasant subject of Brad.

"Have at it," Adam said, gesturing toward her.

"First, since we're both aware that Jazmine's busy playing matchmaker, it seems the best defense is to be honest with each other." She half expected an argument.

"I agree."

He seemed utterly relaxed; in contrast, Shana's nerves were as tight as an overwound guitar string.

"Okay," she said, taking a deep breath. "I think you're wonderful with Jazmine and…and mildly attractive." The man already had an overblown ego and she wasn't about to give him any encouragement.

"Really?" He perked up at that.

"Yes," she admitted reluctantly, "and there are probably a few other positive traits I could add."

He checked his watch. "I have time."

She ignored him. "But without going into why I feel a relationship between us wouldn't work—"

"Aren't you being a little hasty?" he asked without allowing her to finish.

"No," she insisted. "Besides, I'm not interested." She wondered if a big red neon light spelling *liar* was flashing over her head. She *was* interested, but she suspected this whole attraction thing was just the result of being on the rebound. She needed to take it slow, ease into another relationship. Letting Adam Kennedy sweep her off her feet was definitely a bad idea.

He stared at her blankly. "Interested in what?"

"You. I don't mean to be blunt or rude, but I felt I should be clear about that."

"No problem." He shrugged, his expression unchanged.

"I didn't mean to offend you."

"You didn't," he assured her and he certainly didn't look put off by her confession.

"It's just that this isn't the right time for me to get involved," she rushed to add, confused now and more than a little embarrassed. She wished she'd thought this through more carefully. "I've only had the business a short while, and all my energy and resources are tied up in it."

"Of course. That makes perfect sense."

"This has nothing to do with you personally." She was only digging herself in deeper now but couldn't seem to stop.

"Shana, it's not a problem. Don't worry, okay? If anything, it's a relief."

"It is?" she blurted out.

"We should keep each other informed," he murmured. "Just like you suggested. Jazmine is a sweet kid, but we both need to be aware of her game plan."

"Exactly." She felt guilty about the things she'd said. "I hope I didn't offend you—sometimes my tongue goes faster than my brain."

"Not at all," he told her patiently.

"Good." It was probably ridiculous to be so worried about a nine-year-old's scheme and even more ridiculous to mention it to Adam. Thankfully he'd taken everything with a sense of humor.

"Uncle Adam!" Jazmine skated into the parlor and at one glance from Shana, sat down and removed her skates. "Are you done yet? Can we leave now?"

"In a minute."

"Great!" Jazmine looked about as happy as Shana could remember seeing her. "School's out for the year." She slipped on her tennis shoes without bothering to tie them.

Shana's cheeks still burned with embarrassment and she was eager to see Adam and Jazmine leave. "You guys have a great time," she mumbled. "Bye."

Adam slid off the stool and with Jazmine at his side, they ambled out. After the door closed, Shana felt oddly depressed, although she couldn't name the precise reason. She didn't want to analyze it, either.

Business was slow for a Saturday, but experience told Shana it would pick up around lunchtime. She had two part-time employees now in addition to Catherine, the retired woman the Olsens had recommended, who was Shana's most valuable employee. She moved easily between the ice-cream section and the pizza parlor, and she was fully capable of taking over if Shana wanted time off, which was reassuring. This was the one buffer

Shana felt she needed now that she was Jazmine's guardian.

Around eleven, the young father Jazmine had talked to a few weeks earlier stepped into the restaurant. He was without his kids today. He strolled up to the pizza counter; from there he could see Shana in the kitchen, where she was busy stirring a vat of soup. She'd discovered a brand of concentrated soups that tasted as good as homemade and was pleased with the results.

"Hi," he said casually, leaning against the counter.

"Can I help you?" Shana pretended not to remember him, which was the exact opposite of the way she treated her other customers. She worked hard at remembering people's names and creating a warm and welcoming atmosphere. She knew his, too—Tim—but refused to acknowledge it.

"I was wondering if you'd be interested in dinner and a movie."

His invitation took her completely off guard. "I—I beg your pardon?"

"I…well, actually, I was asking you out on a date." His voice was a monotone now, as if she'd deflated his ego, and Shana instantly felt bad.

"I'm flattered, but—"

"Your niece mentioned that you're single, and well, so am I and I was wondering, you know, if you'd like to go out sometime."

Shana wasn't sure what to say. She hesitated, and then decided she could only be honest. "Thank you. I'm flattered that you'd ask, but I just don't have time to date right now." She motioned around her. "This is a new venture for me and I…have to be here."

He frowned. "Is there any particular reason you don't want to go out with me?"

A couple of dozen quickly presented themselves but Shana couldn't manage to get out a single one. "You seem very nice, but—"

"It's the kids, isn't it?"

"No, not at all," she hurried to assure him. "It's like I told you—the timing is wrong." That was the excuse she'd used with Adam; it was also the truth. She'd untangled herself from one relationship and wasn't ready to get involved in another.

"You mean I should've waited until you were finished for the day?"

"No…"

He wiped his face. "You'll have to excuse me. I'm new at this. My wife, I mean ex-wife, and I met in high school and well, it just didn't work out. I don't blame her. We were both too young, but Heather's the only woman I've ever dated and—I don't know what the hell I'm doing." He looked completely crestfallen by the time he'd finished.

Shana felt even worse. "Under other circumstances, I'd be happy to—" She stopped, afraid she'd just make matters worse if she continued. "Would you like a cup of coffee?"

He nodded and sat down on the stool. "That would be great, thanks."

"It's Tim, right?"

He smiled dejectedly. "I'm surprised you remember."

He'd be shocked at everything she did recall about the last time he'd been in the ice-cream parlor—even if she preferred not to.

Shana made them each an espresso, double shot. If he didn't need it she did. When she set the tiny cups on the counter, Tim reached for his wallet. Raising her hand, she said, "It's on the house."

"Thanks."

She waved off his gratitude. For reasons she didn't want to examine too closely, she felt guiltier than ever for rejecting him.

"Can you tell me what I did wrong?" he asked after the first tentative sip.

"It isn't you," she said earnestly. "It really is because of the timing. My new business and looking after my niece and everything."

Over the next three hours, she heard the story of Tim's ten-year marriage and every detail of his divorce. The only time he paused was when she was bombarded with questions from customers or staff, or if the capable Catherine needed her assistance.

She also learned practically the entire story of Tim's life. He seemed to need a willing ear and she provided it, between serving ice cream in three dozen different flavors.

"You know, Tim, it seems to me you're still in love with your wife," she commented while he was on his third espresso.

His eyes flared and he adamantly shook his head. "No way."

"Sorry, but that's how I see it."

"You're wrong."

"Could be, but it's obvious you're crazy about your kids."

He had no argument with that. "They're fabulous."

"So—what else can I do for you?" she asked when he showed no sign of leaving anytime within the foreseeable future.

"You could always go to dinner with me," he suggested.

Shana laughed, knowing she'd be in for a repeat of his disagreement with the divorce attorney. She gave him an A for effort, though. "I thought we already went over that."

"Are you sure you mean no?" he asked again.

"If the lady says no, that's what she means," Adam Kennedy said from the doorway leading into the restaurant. He glared at Tim as if he wanted to teach him a lesson. His tone was friendly enough, but his demeanor wasn't. Shana sighed in exasperation. She was all too aware of the interest Catherine and the others were taking in this little scene. Tim was harmless, his self-esteem in shreds following his divorce, and he was counting on Shana to boost his confidence.

"Thank you very much, Adam," she said tightly, fighting the temptation to say a great deal more, "but the lady can answer for herself."

To her surprise Jazmine laughed outright. "Hello, Mr. Gilmore, remember me?"

Tim looked as if he didn't know what to say. He got off the stool. "I guess it's time to go."

"Sounds like a good idea to me," Adam murmured.

"Adam," Shana chastised, but his gaze didn't waver from Tim's face.

As soon as the other man was out the door, Shana whirled on Adam. "That was completely unnecessary and uncalled for," she said, trying to keep her voice down in deference to her staff and customers.

Adam looked away. "Perhaps, but I wanted to be sure he got the message."

"And what exactly is the message?" Shana demanded.

Adam grinned as if the answer should be obvious.

"Hands off," Jazmine supplied. "You're already spoken for."

* * *

With her shift over, Ali went to check on Commander Dillon one last time and discovered he was asleep. His face was turned toward her and in slumber his features had relaxed. He looked younger than she'd first assumed.

As she stood there, Ali hesitated, resisting the urge to move closer. She longed to place her hand on his arm, to touch him and feel the warmth of his skin. A chill ran down her spine as she remembered he didn't want her anywhere near him. That had been made abundantly clear during her last visit.

She wished she had someone she could talk to about the way she felt. This wasn't something she could discuss with the other women on board. She could be putting her career in jeopardy. Any hint of a romantic entanglement, and she could be in more trouble than she wanted to consider.

Before she left, Ali logged on to her computer.

Sent: June 20
From: Alison.Karas@woodrowwilson.navy.mil
To: Shana@mindsprung.com
Subject: Hello!

Dear Shana,

Just wanted to see how you're doing this week. I think of you and Jazmine every day. I'm doing well myself. We had an emergency appendectomy this week—Commander Dillon. I might have mentioned him before. Before he went under, he seemed to think he might not make it, and asked if I'd look after his affairs. I told him I would, but thankfully that wasn't necessary. He's recuperating nicely now. I think he's

Ali hesitated, remembering the intense look in Frank's eyes as he confessed he had no family. What a lonely life he must lead. Divorced and his brother dead. It didn't sound as if his parents were still living, either. He'd wanted her to dispose of his earthly goods by giving whatever he had to charity. Ali told herself he didn't have time to ask anyone else; she'd been handy, so he'd reached out to her. Still, she sensed that he trusted her. They were basically strangers but he felt he could speak to her and that she would follow through with whatever he'd requested. Had it been necessary, she would have.

After a moment's hesitation, Shana returned to her e-mail. She deleted the last three words and began a new paragraph.

Jazmine mentioned that Adam was stopping by on Saturday. How did that go? I know you think my daughter's trying to match the two of you up and I agree she has no business doing that. But the truth is, I don't think it's such a bad idea.

Adam is a good man and while you might have a dozen excuses not to recognize what a find he is, look again. This is your big sister talking here. I mean it: take a close look at this guy. Adam is easy on the eyes (nice but not essential), he's intelligent and hard-working and wonderful with kids.

I just hope keeping Jazmine for the next six months will convince you that you want children of your own.

I can tell how close the two of you are getting just from the e-mails. It's almost enough to make me jealous!

Your e-mails mean the world to me. Keep them coming.

Love,
Ali

It didn't take long for Ali to get a response. She wasn't sure if it was because of the time difference or if she happened to catch her sister at the computer.

Sent: June 21
From: Shana@mindsprung.com
To: Alison.Karas@woodrowwilson.navy.mil
Subject: Commander, you say?

Dear Ali,

No, you didn't mention anyone named Commander Dillon. What gives? Is he all right? I assume he must be. But the fact that you're saying anything at all tells me you're interested in him. This is a development worth watching. I know, I know, all shipboard romances are strictly taboo. But tell me more!

I'm afraid I made an idiot of myself in front of Adam this morning. Trust me, any romantic interest he might have felt toward me is deader than roadkill. I'm such a fool.

All right, all right, I'll tell you what I did, but you've got to promise not to mention it again. I decided he should be aware of Jazmine's little scheme. That seems only fair, don't you think?

In retrospect, I still feel it needed to be said but maybe I didn't handle it in the best possible way. When I assured him I wasn't interested in him, I came off sounding like…I don't know what. I keep saying it, but this isn't the right time for me to get involved. It really isn't, not with just starting this business.

And guess what? Another guy, who was recently divorced, came in later this afternoon and asked me out. I turned him down using the same excuse and felt terrible. (By the way, it's thanks to the little matchmaker that he knew I was single.)

Oh, and did I mention Brad phoned? Let me tell you that was a short conversation. If I needed confirmation that I did the right thing in breaking up with him, our conversation was it.

Hearing from you is wonderful. Both Jazmine and I miss you terribly. I never realized how much effort went into being a parent. Don't get me wrong, Jazz is one fabulous kid and I'm crazy about her, but I didn't have any idea how much my life would change when she came to live with me.

You're right, Ali, I'm absolutely certain now that I want to be a mother one day. That's a bit intimidating, though. With everything that's happened in the last few months, I've pushed all thoughts of another relationship out of my mind. I still think I need to wait a while. Is that a biological clock I hear ticking? Not to worry, I have plenty of time. Lots of women have children when they're in their mid or even late thirties these days.

Nevertheless, I need a while to clear my head. Adam's attractive, for sure, and I might be interested in Tim if he wasn't so hung up on his ex-wife. (Tim's the divorced father I mentioned earlier.)

Write back soon and tell me more about this commander guy. He sounds like one of those mucky-muck officers. Is that good or bad?

Love ya,
Shana

Ali read the e-mail through twice and discovered she was smiling when she finished. She wasn't going to give up on Shana and Adam just yet.

Chapter Eleven

"It's summer," Jazmine announced the first Monday after the end of school. "Uncle Adam's got three days off. We should all do something special to celebrate."

Shana hated to discourage Jazmine's enthusiasm, but she couldn't leave her restaurant on a whim. "Do something?" she repeated. "Like what?"

That was all the invitation Jazmine needed. She hopped onto the barstool and rested her arms on the counter. "When my dad was stationed in Italy, he took me to Florence right after school was out. We had so much fun, and I saw Michelangelo's David. It's really cool, you know?"

"We have some interesting museums in the area," Shana suggested, but her heart wasn't in it. Given her druthers, of which she had few, she would opt to visit Victoria, British Columbia. She'd heard it was a lovely city and very English in style.

Jazmine sighed and shook her head. "I've been to dozens of museums, but that feels too much like a school outing. This should be *special*."

"What about an amusement park?" Perhaps on Sunday Shana could stuff herself into a swimsuit, make Jazmine promise not to take her picture, and they could head for the local water park.

Again Jazmine was less than excited. "I suppose, but I'm looking for something that's not so…ordinary. Everyone goes to parks. This is a celebration. I survived a new school, made friends and Aunt Shana's still speaking to me." She giggled as she said this, and Shana laughed, too.

"We had a bit of a rough start," Shana acknowledged.

"It took me a while to adjust," Jazmine admitted in turn. "Uncle Adam helped me."

"With what, exactly?" She recalled the backpack advice, and the fact that he'd apparently told her to stop matchmaking—hadn't he?—but she didn't know what else he'd said.

"Never mind." Jazmine slid off the barstool. "That's an idea—I'll call Uncle Adam."

"To do what?" Shana asked, but her question went unanswered as Jazmine hurried toward the phone.

"You should take a day just for the two of you," Catherine suggested, apparently listening in on their conversation. "You've been here nearly every day for weeks."

"New business-owners don't take days off," Shana said. It was true that she'd spent every day at the restaurant, although she'd taken brief breaks and nearly one whole Sunday the week before. She'd felt like a new woman afterward. The thought of one entire twenty-four hour period when she didn't have her hands in pizza dough or her face in a three-gallon container of ice cream sounded heavenly. Getting away was just the respite she needed.

"It isn't for you as much as your niece," Catherine continued. "Kind of a reward for doing so well."

Shana knew she was right. Against the odds, Jazmine had succeeded in adapting to a new school and a new home, and she'd made friends.

A few minutes later, Jazmine set the phone aside and raced over to Shana. "Uncle Adam suggested visiting Victoria, B.C.," she said breathlessly. "I've never been there and he said it's a wonderful day trip."

"That does sound nice," Shana said wistfully. She was astonished at the way Adam's suggestion reflected her own earlier musings about Victoria. It was almost eerie.

"He wants to talk to you," Jazmine said. She ran to get the portable phone and handed it to Shana.

Shana walked into the back room, nervously tucking a strand of hair behind her ear. She'd moussed it into submission that morning, but whole sections were already attempting a breakout.

"Hello," she said and hoped her voice didn't betray her feelings. She thought about this man far too often and had an intense love-hate relationship with him that he knew nothing about. She was attracted to him and yet she didn't want to be. The fact that he—

"Shana?" Adam said, cutting into her thoughts.

"I'm here," she said primly.

"That's a great idea of Jazmine's. You can come, can't you?"

"To Victoria, you mean? Ah…"

"We'll make it a day trip. I'm off until Thursday. I'll pick you and Jazmine up, then we'll take the Fauntleroy ferry over to the Kitsap Peninsula, drive to Port Angeles and take another ferry across the Strait to Victoria."

"I…I'm—" Shana hesitated when she saw Jazmine staring at her with pleading eyes. She'd folded her hands as if in prayer, and Shana's resolve weakened. "I'll need to check with Catherine before I take a whole day." Shana instantly felt guilty; she'd invested her life savings in this business and she shouldn't be running off for a day of fun. She should be at work.

"Ask her," Adam urged.

Shana turned away from the phone and came face-to-face with Catherine, who had her hands on her hips. "Go. I'll manage just fine. It's only one day, for Pete's sake."

"But…"

"Aunt Shana," Jazmine said pulling on her arm. "Just do it. We'll have a blast."

Shana wasn't nearly as sure. That night, long after Jazmine was in bed and she herself should have been, she e-mailed her sister.

Sent: June 24
From: Shana@mindsprung.com
To: Alison.Karas@woodrowwilson.navy.mil
Subject: Jazmine, Adam Kennedy and me

Dear Alison,

As you probably already know, I'm going off on a day trip to Victoria, British Columbia, with Jazz and Adam. Basically I got talked into it, and I'll give you three guesses whose fault that is. Your daughter could talk circles around Larry King. Mark my words, that kid will have her own talk show one day.

Yes, Adam Kennedy will be there, too. I don't mind having him around anymore. I put up a good fight, let him know I wasn't interested in a relationship and even made a point of telling him about Jazz playing matchmaker. He listened politely and agreed with everything I had to say. The least he could've done was argue—just kidding! Without even trying, he's worn down my defenses. I have to admit I've enjoyed the time I've spent with him. Twice now, after he's visited Jazz, he's stayed for a cup of coffee and we've talked. There hasn't been a hint of romance, although, yes—I'm attracted. I definitely feel we have some chemistry, but I'm too preoccupied (and too scared!) to do anything about it.

Okay, I've bared my soul. It's your turn. What's up with you and this Commander Dillon? I know you, Ali. You wouldn't have mentioned him at all if you didn't care, so I repeat—what's up?

It's almost eleven and I should be in bed. Adam's arriving very early. I offered to drive over to his place, but he said it was no trouble coming to get us.

Write soon. Jazmine and I both look forward to your e-mails.

Love,
Shana

* * *

Less than twelve hours later, Shana was on a mid-morning ferry that had left Port Angeles for Vancouver Island. An excited Jazmine jogged up and down the outside deck while Adam and Shana drank cups of coffee inside. They were seated on wooden benches, across from each other.

"I can't believe I'm doing this," she muttered. The alarm had rung at four that morning and they were on the road by five.

"Did you see the Olympic Mountains?" Jazmine dashed inside shouting—as if they could possibly have missed them. "I learned in class that some of those mountains have never been climbed or explored."

This was news to Shana, but she wasn't much of an expert on Washington State history or geography.

"Do either of you know about Point Roberts?" Adam asked when Jazmine threw herself down on the bench, sitting next to Adam and across from Shana.

Both Shana and Jazmine shook their heads. "Never heard of it," Shana said.

"It's a little piece of the United States that is geographically part of Canada."

"What?" Jazmine frowned. "I don't get it."

"The United States and Canada are separated by the 49th parallel at Washington and British Columbia. There's a small point of land that drops below it. That's Point Roberts. Maybe we can go there sometime."

"So it's in Canada but not really?"

"Take a look at a map and you'll see what I mean."

While Jazmine walked over to examine the wall at the other end of the ferry, where a map of Washington was posted, Shana sipped her coffee and smiled at Adam. "She idolizes you, you know."

Adam shifted on the hard bench and crossed his arms. "As it happens, I think the world of her, too."

It was confession time for Shana, although what she had to say was probably no secret to Adam. "I was jealous of that in the beginning."

Adam's gaze held hers. "And now?"

"Now..." She hesitated. "I appreciate the fact that she has you. She needs a strong male figure in her life, especially with her dad gone."

"She's come to love you, too, Shana. And it's all happened in remarkably little time. That says a lot for you, I think. You've been patient with her and you've managed to find just the right approach."

His praise brought a sheen of tears to her eyes. Embarrassed and wanting to hide the effect of his words, Shana quickly blinked them away.

"Listen," Adam said, lowering his voice. "There's something I should probably tell you. There's a rumor floating around that several of us could be transferred to Hawaii. I've wanted to go back for quite a while— ever since I left, really. I just wish the timing was better. I should also tell you it could be soon."

"No," Shana cried, unable to hold back the automatic protest.

Everyone in the immediate vicinity seemed to stop and look in their direction.

Adam leaned forward and reached for her hand. "Dare I hope that response is for you as well as Jazmine?"

Shana ignored the question. "I guess I should congratulate you, then—since this is an assignment you want."

"What about you, Shana?" he pressed. "Will you miss me?"

He wasn't going to drop this as easily as she'd hoped. "Of…course." The lump in her throat was growing as she dealt with the coming disappointment—her own and Jazmine's. This would devastate her niece.

"I'll miss you and Jazmine, too." Adam's eyes held hers, and he brushed his thumb over her hand. "I've enjoyed our visits. Especially those talks over coffee."

As the old expression had it, hope sprang eternal. "It's not a for-sure decision, right? I mean, there's a possibility you won't be going."

"I wouldn't count on it."

"Oh, well," she said, doing her best to seem nonchalant about this unexpected turn of events. He'd probably known for some time and was only now free to mention it. "I guess that answers that." She tried to speak lightly, concealing her sense of loss.

He grinned sheepishly. "I have to admit that Jazmine's matchmaking plans didn't upset me nearly as much as they did you."

Her responding smile felt a little shaky, which was exactly how she felt herself. During the last few weeks, she'd come to like and trust Adam, and just when she was feeling comfortable with him, he made this announcement.

Adam switched seats so that he was sitting next to her. "I probably shouldn't have said anything about Hawaii yet, but I wanted you to know as soon as possible, so we can prepare Jazmine."

"No—you did the right thing." Until she'd learned that he might leave, Shana hadn't realized how much she'd come to rely on Adam. She and Jazmine would be on their own for the next four and a half months, and just then that felt like an eternity.

"Hey, guys," Jazmine said, running toward them. She flopped down on the wooden seat. "I found Point Roberts on the map! It's really cool, isn't it?"

"Really cool," Adam agreed solemnly.

Shana didn't know how a whole day could pass so quickly. Victoria was everything she'd heard and read. Although she'd never been to England, she imagined it must be like this. They explored the harbor, rode a horse-drawn carriage through the downtown area, had high tea at the Empress Hotel and toured some quaint little shops. In one of them, Shana couldn't resist buying a made-in-England teapot covered in delicate little roses, while Adam got each of them a sweatshirt with maple leaves dancing across the front.

"I loved the carriage ride best," Jazmine told them on the ferry ride back to Port Angeles. "I wish we had time to visit Butchart Gardens." She waved a brochure she'd picked up. "The pictures of the flowers are so beautiful. I always wanted a garden…." She leaned her head against Shana and closed her eyes. Within moments she was asleep.

Shana carefully eased the girl off her shoulder and gently laid Jazmine's head down on the seat. Lifting the girl's legs, she set them on the bench, then covered Jazmine with her jacket. Her niece looked angelic, and Shana's heart swelled with love for this child. She felt protective and proud. Jazmine had taught her so many lessons about love.

Adam slid over so Shana could sit with him across

from Jazmine. The day had been wonderful but, like Jazmine, she was tired. When Adam placed his arm around her, she gave in to the urge to rest her head against his shoulder. It was an invitation to intimacy, she realized, and she relaxed, comfortable and suddenly happy. "Thank you for such a special day," she whispered as he twined their fingers together.

His hold on her tightened momentarily.

Shana turned her head to look up at him—and that was when it happened. She read the intention in his eyes and knew he wanted to kiss her. At first, she wondered if what she saw was a reflection of her own desire, but instinct told her he felt the same thing. For the briefest of moments, she had a choice—she could either pull away or let him kiss her. Without rational thought, she closed her eyes, lifted her mouth to his and accepted his kiss. As soon as their lips met, Shana knew she'd made the right decision. She felt his kiss all the way to her toes.

His lips glided over hers in a slow, sensual exploration that had her nerves quivering. Luckily she was seated; otherwise she was sure her knees would have given out on her. Then his hands were in her hair, his fingers splayed as he positioned his mouth over hers. When he finally eased away, she needed a moment to regain her composure.

"Wow," Adam whispered.

"You can say that again," Shana said, still caught up in the feelings his touch had aroused.

Adam slowly expelled his breath. "Okay, now what?" His eyes burned into hers, as if seeking answers to questions she had yet to form.

"Now…" Shana hesitated. "Now we know."

"Do you want to play this by ear?"

She pressed her forehead against his chest. "I'm not sure I've had enough piano lessons."

Adam grinned and kissed the top of her head. "Don't worry, I'm in no rush. We'll take this one step at a time."

"First piano lessons, and now we're out on the dance floor. Can't you just hold me for a few minutes and leave it at that?"

"For now."

For now, that was enough. As far as anything else was concerned, she'd have to see what her heart told her.

Chapter Twelve

Ali read her daughter's e-mail a second time and smiled.

Sent: June 26
From: Jazmine@mindsprung.com
To: Alison.Karas@woodrowwilson.navy.mil
Subject: Guess what I saw

Hi Mom,

I had a great day and my favorite things were the carriage (our horse was named Silver) and having tea in a fancy hotel and watching Uncle Adam try to fit his finger in the handle of a little china cup. On the ferry home Uncle Adam and Aunt Shana sat next to each other and I was mostly asleep. They got real quiet and so I peeked and guess what? THEY WERE KISS-ING. Didn't I tell you they were falling in love? I knew because Uncle Adam comes by almost every day he has off now.

It gets even better. On the drive home, Aunt Shana had her head on his shoulder and then she didn't when I pretended to wake up. They were whispering a lot, too. I tried not to listen, but I couldn't help it. They were talking about Hawaii and I think it might be where they want to spend their honeymoon. Is this cool, or what?

Love ya,
Jazz

Ali leaned back in her desk chair, feeling satisfied and more than a little cheered. Her daughter was full of news about the romance between Adam and Shana, and gladly accepted credit for it. She seemed convinced that Shana and Adam were just days away from an engage-ment—or maybe an elopement. That certainly wasn't the impression Shana gave her, but she could see real change in her sister's attitude toward Adam.

In their last conversation, before Alison flew out of Seattle, Shana had told her she'd completely sworn off men. Apparently she'd reconsidered. This time, how-ever, Shana had found herself a winner. Adam was as different from Brad as snow was from sun, and Ali hoped her sister realized it.

Her first indication of the possible romance had been the e-mail Shana had sent full of questions about Adam. Several more had followed the original; all had thinly veiled inquiries about him. Shana had become more open and honest, admitting she felt an attraction even if she hadn't decided what to do about it. Despite that, Alison saw the evidence of a growing relationship with every e-mail.

Glancing at her watch, she turned off her computer. It was time to relieve Rowland in medical. As she checked her schedule, her gaze fell on her wedding band and she paused. Should she switch it to her right hand—or remove it entirely? She wanted to pass it on to Jazmine one day. Slipping the ring off her finger, she held it in the palm of her hand, weighing her options. No, she wasn't ready to give it up yet. She placed it on her right hand, instead.

The very fact that she'd questioned wearing her wedding band was a sign. She would always love Peter but her life with him was over. She supposed her uncertainty about the ring had something to do with Commander Dillon, too. She didn't want him to believe she was married, but it might be safest if he did…. Still, moving the ring that represented her love for Peter to her right hand was a compromise.

As far as she could tell, this feeling of hers for Frank Dillon was completely one-sided. If he'd noticed her lately, he hadn't given the tiniest hint. He couldn't. One thing she knew about Commander Dillon was that he lived and breathed for the Navy. He wouldn't go against regulations if his life depended on it, and Alison wouldn't want him to. But it made for an uncomfortable situation as they pretended there was nothing between them. Perhaps there wasn't. She couldn't be sure, but in her heart she felt there was.

Commander Dillon was still recuperating in sick bay. He hated it, longed to get back to work and he was undeniably a pain in the butt. Her colleagues made their feelings known on a daily basis, but Alison simply didn't acknowledge his bad moods. As a result, the cantankerous commander didn't know what to think of her, and that was just fine with Ali.

While others avoided him, she saw as much of him as her busy schedule would allow, which was never longer than a few minutes at a time. Her feelings for him grew more intense with each day.

When she stepped into the infirmary, Lieutenant Rowland handed her his notes. "You're welcome to the beast," he muttered under his breath. "He's been in a hell of a mood all day. Doc says he'll have him out this week, but I don't think that's near soon enough to suit the commander."

That went without saying. When he'd first arrived at the infirmary Frank Dillon had been in agony, which meant his attitude was docile—at least compared to his current frame of mind. After reading Rowland's notations, Alison pulled back the curtain surrounding him. The commander sat up in bed, arms folded across his chest. He scowled when he saw her.

"You've become a rather disagreeable patient, Commander."

"I want out of here," he barked.

"That's no reason to yell. I believe you've made your wishes quite clear."

He narrowed his gaze.

"As it happens, Commander, you aren't the one making the decisions. You can huff and puff all you want, but it isn't going to do you a bit of good." She reached for his wrist and found his pulse elevated. Little wonder, seeing how agitated he was.

"How much longer is this going to take?" he demanded gruffly.

As the lieutenant had reported, their patient was in a foul mood. Having her around hadn't eased his temper, either. "I understand you'll be released this week," she said as she lowered the bed so that he was flat on his back. She needed to examine his incision. By now he knew the procedure as well as she did.

Ali carefully peeled back the bandage to check for any sign of infection. With the tips of her fingers she gently tested the area while the commander stared impatiently at the ceiling.

"This is healing nicely," she assured him.

"Then let me get back to work."

"It isn't my decision."

He sounded as if he was grinding his teeth in frustration. "I can't stand wasting time like this," he growled.

"Can I help in some way?" she asked, thinking she could find him a book or a deck of cards.

"Yes," he shouted, "you can get me out of here!"

"You know I can't do that," she said reasonably. "Only a physician can discharge you."

"I've got to do something before I go stir-crazy." He grimaced with pain as he attempted to sit up.

"Commander, you're not helping matters."

He glared at her as though she was personally responsible for this torture. "Just go. Get out of my sight. I don't want you around anymore, understand?"

She hesitated. "I'm responsible for your care."

"Get someone else."

"Commander," she tried again, but he cut her off.

"Get out!" He pointed at her. "And that's an order."

Alison swallowed down the hurt as she walked out of his cubicle. His words, harsh and vindictive, rang in her ears during the rest of her shift. He didn't want her anywhere near him and he wasn't afraid to say so. Her stomach twisted in a knot, and she felt like a fool for having made assumptions about mutual feelings that obviously didn't exist. Not on his part, anyway.

She didn't blame Frank for wanting to be back on duty, but he'd taken all his resentment and anger out on her. That wasn't fair, and it added to the hurt Alison felt.

Silently she watched as the corpsman delivered his dinner tray. Dillon glanced at her, then turned away, as if he found the sight of her repugnant.

Thirty minutes later, when she walked past, she noticed that he'd barely touched his meal. She considered reminding him that he'd need his strength, but he wouldn't want to hear it. And she wasn't willing to risk another tongue-lashing.

Twice more during the course of her shift, Ali resisted the urge to check on him. Frank had been very explicit about the fact that he didn't want her company.

When she'd finished, she returned to her quarters and curled up on her bed. After her shift she usually wrote Jazmine and her sister, but not tonight. Instead she reviewed the conversation with Frank.

She told herself it was silly to have her feelings hurt by his rudeness, that he didn't mean it, but she couldn't help taking it personally. Earlier she'd always shrugged off his abrasive manner, and she couldn't understand why today was so different. Probably because she'd let her attraction to him get out of hand.

Ali wouldn't be surprised if he was released the next

morning, which was just as well. In a little more than four months, she reminded herself, she'd be home with her daughter and soon after that she'd be a civilian. This was an unsettling thought because Ali loved the Navy, but her resignation was necessary. Jazmine needed her, and Alison had given the Navy all she had to give, including her husband.

As she'd suspected, Commander Dillon was released the following morning. Alison hated that his last words to her had been spoken in anger, but she tried to forget it. She wished him good health, but he was out of her life now, and it was unlikely they'd see each other again. Perhaps in another time or place they might have made a relationship work. But not here and not now.

Of more interest was the romance developing between her sister and Adam Kennedy, and as soon as she could, Alison logged on to the computer to check her e-mail. She could count on hearing from Jazmine at least once a day.

To her delight, there was an e-mail from Adam, too, but as she read it, her pleasure quickly evaporated. Adam feared that now his shoulder had healed, he was about to be transferred. He'd told Shana, but didn't have the heart to mention it to Jazmine until he got his papers. Almost in passing, he added how much he'd enjoyed getting to know Shana.

This was dreadful! Jazmine would be devastated if Adam was transferred out of the area, and she wasn't the only one. Shana was going to be just as disappointed.

With a heavy heart she read her daughter's chatty e-mail next.

Sent: June 30
From: Jazmine@mindsprung.com
To: Alison.Karas@woodrowwilson.navy.mil
Subject: Update—sort of

Hi Mom,

Aunt Shana said we could plant a garden! She said
we could grow vegetables and flowers. I don't want
to plant green beans because then I might have to
eat them. Zucchini would be all right, though. Will
you give Aunt Shana your recipe for baked zucchini?
Tell her to add more cheese than what the recipe
calls for, okay? You had a good recipe for green peppers, too, didn't you? I could even eat those raw, but
I like them better stuffed.

I think a garden will be lots of fun, don't you? Uncle
Adam said he'd help. Isn't that great?

See you soon.

Love,
Jazmine

Alison didn't know where Shana would find time to
start a garden. As it was, her sister worked from dawn
to dusk, but the plans for this latest project showed her
how hard Shana was trying with Jazmine. Somehow, the
two of them had managed to talk Adam into helping.
How much he could do was questionable, since he

couldn't risk damaging his shoulder again, but he seemed a willing participant.

The last e-mail came from onboard ship. Not until she opened it did she see that it was from Commander Dillon. Ali stared at his name for a moment before she read his message. Five words said it all. *Thank you for your excellent care. Commander Frank Dillon.*

"No," she whispered. "Thank *you,* Commander." She had much to be grateful for. Because even if this was as far as it went, Frank had shown her that her heart was still alive.

Sheer weakness had prompted him to send Alison Karas that e-mail, Frank thought as he returned to his stateroom at the end of his shift. Frank was not a weak man, and he was irritated with himself for more reasons than he wanted to count.

He knew he wasn't a good patient. He just couldn't tolerate lying around in bed all day. He wanted to be back on the job, doing what he enjoyed most, contributing his skills where they were needed. If his appendix was going to give out on him, he would've preferred it to happen while they were in port.

The worst part of his ordeal wasn't his ruptured appendix and the subsequent surgery. That he'd come through with only minor difficulties. But he wasn't sure he would survive Lieutenant Commander Karas. After all these years on his own, without female companionship, committed to the Navy, he was finally attracted to a woman. *Strongly* attracted. She invaded his dreams and haunted his waking moments. Every day for damn near a week she'd been at his bedside.

He didn't like it. Just when his mind had started to clear and his system was free of those drugs they'd given him, he saw something he hadn't noticed earlier. *Her wedding ring.* It shook him.

That first time they met, Alison Karas hadn't denied being married and she'd worn a wedding ring—on her left hand. He stared at the computer screen. *Married.* He'd forgotten about it until this week. Then, when he'd remembered—and realized he was fantasizing about a married woman—he'd lost it. Even worse, she'd moved the ring to her right hand. What did *that* say about her?

He'd been impatient to get back to his duties before, but after he saw that wedding band, he was downright desperate to escape the infirmary. *There's no fool like an old fool*, as they said.

His anger had turned on Alison and he wanted her as far away from him as possible. Later he regretted that outburst. She'd done nothing to deserve his tongue-lashing. But he found it difficult to be civil, and all because he'd realized there was no hope of any kind of relationship, let alone a permanent one.

He could accept that, but he wasn't a man who enjoyed temptation and this woman definitely fit that description. Still, he felt compelled to apologize for his rudeness. Seeing her again was out of the question, so he'd decided to send an e-mail. He wrote a dozen versions before he settled on the brief and simple message, then hit Send before he could change his mind.

For better or worse, she had it now, and that was the

end of it. He made his way to the first deck and lifting his head he scanned the horizon. All that stretched before him was ocean—a huge blue expanse of emptiness. He saw his life like that and it bothered him.

Until now, it never had.

Chapter Thirteen

Adam was charmed by Jazmine's excitement about their little garden. He'd managed to find someone to turn over a small patch at the back of Shana's rental house. Then Jazmine and her aunt had planted neat rows of red-leaf lettuce, peas, green peppers and three varieties of tomato. Although they'd been warned by the man at the local nursery, they'd purchased a number of zucchini plants, too. Apparently it did exceptionally well in the Seattle area and supplied an abundant crop. Jazmine claimed her mother had fabulous recipes for zucchini. Baked zucchini and zucchini bread and something else.

"Around September if you see anyone buying zucchini in the grocery, you'll know that's a person without a friend," the nursery owner had joked as he hauled their plants out to the vehicle.

Once they were back at the house and the plants were in the freshly tilled soil, Adam watched Jazmine with amusement. Every five minutes, the girl was out in the garden checking on the plants' growth, making sure there were no slugs in the vicinity. God help them if they were. Just to be on the safe side, she carried a salt shaker.

The flower beds—well, they were another story. He'd lost track of all the seedlings Shana had purchased. Most of them he didn't even recognize. Pink ones and white ones, purple and yellow. They certainly made the yard look colorful. Pretty but... Women and flowers—he never could understand what they found so fascinating. For himself, he thought practical made more sense than pretty, although he hadn't shared that reaction with Shana.

True, he'd had a jade plant once but it died for lack of attention. Shana, predictably, had clusters of house plants—on windowsills and tables—but he couldn't begin to guess what types they were. Knowing Jazmine, he wouldn't have thought she'd be too interested in this kind of thing, either, but apparently he was wrong. The kid loved it as much as Shana did.

"Aunt Shana said she'd be home around eight," Jazmine informed him on Saturday at five. They'd spent a quiet afternoon together. While he watched a Mariners baseball game on television, Jazmine tended the garden. He'd found it relaxing, but he missed being with Shana. He would've stopped at the ice-cream parlor, but he knew that Saturdays, especially in summer, tended to be busy.

Jazmine had patiently watered the rows of newly planted seedlings, being careful not to oversaturate the soil. She'd examined every inch to check for weeds and had ruthlessly yanked up a number of small green plants; Adam suspected they were actually vegetables.

He glanced up from the post-game analysis and saw that Jazmine was standing in front of him. "We should make dinner," she announced. "A real, proper dinner."

"We?" he muttered. In case Jazmine hadn't noticed, he wasn't the domestic type. Besides he had to protect his shoulder. Every meal in the last few weeks had come out of a microwave or in a pizza box.

"We could do it," Jazmine insisted, as if putting together a three-course meal was no trouble at all.

"Really? I wouldn't mind getting takeout. Or maybe Shana could bring home a pizza. Wouldn't that be easier?"

Frowning, Jazmine shook her head. "She has pizza all the time. Besides, home cooking is better for you."

Adam wondered when she'd become such an expert. "You're sure the two of us can do this?"

"Of course."

Ah, the confidence of the young. Still, Adam had his doubts. "You should know I'm kitchen-challenged."

Jazmine giggled. "I cook a lot. I'll do it."

If Jazmine knew her way around the kitchen, then perhaps this wouldn't be so complicated. He could supervise from in front of the TV.

"You'll have to help, though."

He should've known she wouldn't let him off scot-free. "What do you want me to do?"

"The grocery store won't sell me wine, so you'll have to buy that."

His eyebrows shot up. "Wine?"

Jazmine nodded. "And flowers," she said in a tone that brooked no argument.

"Yes, ma'am. Any particular kind?" He resisted mentioning that there was a yard full of flowers outside, although they were mostly quite small.

"I want you to buy roses and we're going to need candles, too. Tall ones."

"You got it." He bit his tongue to keep from reminding her that it wouldn't be dark until ten. "Should I buy red or white wine?" he asked.

Jazmine stared at him blankly.

"Red generally goes with meat and white wine is served with chicken or fish."

"What goes with everything?"

"Champagne is good."

She grinned then, her decision made. "Buy champagne and make it a big bottle, okay?"

"Have you decided what you're cooking?" he asked.

"Of course I have," she told him scornfully.

"And that would be?"

She sighed, as though she was a master chef dealing with obtuse underlings. "I've decided to cook my specialty."

"Which is?"

"A surprise," she said without pause, using her hands to shoo him out the door. He watched her march into the kitchen. From the corner of his eye, Adam saw her pull several cookbooks off the shelf.

After he'd finished his errands, Adam decided to visit the ice-cream parlor, after all. It was just too hard to stay away. As he'd expected, Shana was doing a robust business. Catherine worked on the pizza side with a young assistant, while Shana and another part-time student served ice cream. They had at least a dozen customers waiting their turn. Adam took a seat and when Shana saw him, she blushed, fussed with her hair, then went back to helping her customers. Her self-conscious reaction pleased him. Ten minutes later, she had a chance to take a break.

After washing her hands, she joined him. "Hi," she said, offering him a shy smile.

He hadn't known there was a shy bone in her body until he'd kissed her. That kiss had been a revelation to him. Their feelings weren't simple or uncomplicated, although he hadn't deciphered the full extent of them yet. He did know their kiss had changed them. Changed their relationship.

He'd been attracted to her from the beginning and was sure she'd felt the same way about him. They'd skirted each other for weeks, both denying the attraction, and then all of a sudden, after that day in Victoria, it was there. Undeniable. Unmistakable. He no longer tried to hide his feelings and she didn't, either.

"Where's Jazmine?" she asked. "In the park?"

He shook his head. "At home, cooking dinner. Her specialty, she says. I don't suppose you have any clue what that might be?"

"You left her alone?" Shana's eyes widened with alarm. "In the kitchen with the stove on? Adam, she's only nine! Sometimes that's hard to remember, but she's still just a kid."

"She seemed perfectly fine," he said, suddenly deciding Shana was right. "She's the one who sent me to the store." He slid out of the booth. "I'll get back now."

Shana sighed, then stretched out one hand and stopped him. "It was good to see you," she said in a low voice.

He gave her hand a small squeeze. "You, too. Don't be late for dinner."

"I won't," she promised.

Once again Adam started toward the door, then paused and turned around. "What's her specialty?"

Shana grinned. "It's probably canned chili with grated cheese on top."

He dismissed that. "I think it might be more involved. Whatever it is requires a cookbook."

Shana's grin faded. "In that case, you'd better hurry."

"I'm on my way."

Shana smiled again, and it reminded him—as if he needed reminding—how attracted he was to her. And just when their relationship was beginning to show real promise, he'd be leaving the Seattle area.

She followed him to the front door. "Any word on that transfer?" she asked.

If he didn't know better, he'd think she'd been reading his mind. "Not yet." It wouldn't be long, though. Hawaii was a dream assignment. Who wouldn't want to be stationed there? With its endless miles of white sandy beaches and sunshine, Hawaii had always appealed to him. Yet Seattle, known for its frequent drizzle and gray skies, was of more interest now than the tropical paradise.

"Did you mention anything about the transfer to Jazmine?" she asked.

He shook his head. He couldn't make himself do it.

"Coward," she muttered.

Adam shrugged lightly. "Guilty as charged."

Shana glanced at her watch. "I'll be leaving in about an hour and a half."

"Okay, I'll let Martha Stewart know." Feeling the need to touch her, he reached for her hand. Even with the restaurant full of customers, they entwined their fingers, and it was a long moment before either of them moved. He felt the urge to take her in his arms and she must have felt the same impulse because she swayed toward him before shaking her head and dropping her hand.

"I should get back to work and you need to get back to Jazmine," she said, her voice little more than a whisper.

"Right."

"Bye." Shana gave him a small wave. Adam heard the reluctance in her voice, a reluctance he shared.

Jazmine met him at the front door, took his bags and banned him from the kitchen. "I can't be disturbed," she said grandly.

Adam turned the television on again and sat with one ankle balanced on his knee, aiming the remote. He couldn't find anything he wanted to watch. "Need any help in there?" he called out.

"No, thanks."

Five minutes later he repeated the offer.

This time Jazmine ignored him, but soon afterward, she asked, "Aunt Shana isn't going to be late, is she?"

"She'd phone," Adam said, and hoped she would.

At three minutes after eight, Shana walked into the house. "I'm home," she said unnecessarily.

Adam stood and Jazmine hurried eagerly out of the kitchen. "I hope you're hungry."

"Famished," she said.

As if on cue, Adam's stomach growled.

With a sweeping gesture of her arm, Jazmine invited them into the kitchen. The table was covered with a tablecloth twice the right size. The cloth brushed the floor, and Adam wondered if she'd used a floral printed sheet. The candles were stuck in empty Coke bottles—apparently she hadn't found real candle-holders—and were positioned on either side of the roses, which she'd arranged in a glass bowl. The effect was surprisingly artful. There were place settings, including wine goblets, in front of the three chairs.

"Jazmine!" Shana exclaimed, hugging her niece. "This is absolutely lovely."

The nine-year-old blushed at the praise and wiped her hands on her apron. "Uncle Adam helped."

"Not much," Adam protested.

"We can start now," she said with authority. "Please light the candles and pour the champagne. I'm having soda in my glass."

He bowed slightly. "At your service."

"Everyone, sit down," Jazmine ordered when he'd finished. She gestured toward the table. "I have an appetizer." Following that announcement, she brought out a bowl of dry Cheerios mixed with peanuts, raisins and pretzels.

"Excellent," Shana said, exchanging a look with Adam. They both struggled to maintain their composure.

"This is only the start," Jazmine promised, flitting about the kitchen like a parrot on the loose. "I made all our favorites—macaroni and cheese, Tater Tots and salad. Uncle Adam, there's no tomatoes in your salad and, Aunt Shana, no croutons on yours."

Shana's eyes met Adam's. "She's paying attention."

"I'll say."

"Plus macaroons for dessert," Jazmine added proudly.

"Macaroons?" Adam repeated.

Jazmine removed the bowl of Cheerios. "Yes, *chocolate* macaroons. Those are my favorites, so no complaining."

It was an odd meal, but Adam had no complaints and neither, apparently, did Shana.

"We'll do the dishes," he said when they'd eaten. The champagne had relaxed him and Shana, too, because they lingered over the last glass while Jazmine moved into the living room.

"This really was sweet of her," Shana whispered.

"Very sweet," Adam agreed. What happened next, he blamed on the champagne. Before he could question the wisdom of it, he leaned close to Shana, intending to kiss her.

She could've stopped him, but didn't. Instead she shut her eyes and leaned toward him, too. The kiss was every bit as good as their first one. No, it was better, Adam decided. In fact, her kisses could fast become addictive—a risk he'd just have to take. He brought his chair closer to Shana's and she gripped his shirt collar as they kissed again.

She pulled away sometime later and pressed her forehead against his. It took him a moment to find his focus. He savored having her close, enjoyed her scent and the way she felt. Jazmine might see them, but he didn't care as long as Shana didn't—and obviously she didn't.

"You two need help in there?" Jazmine called from the living room.

Like guilty teenagers, Shana and Adam broke apart. "We're fine," Shana answered.

Adam wasn't so sure that was true.

Sent: July 6
From: Jazmine@mindsprung.com
To: Alison.Karas@woodrowwilson.navy.mil
Subject: My plan is working

Dear Mom,

I cooked dinner all by myself! You know what I like best about Uncle Adam? He doesn't treat me like a kid. He spent Saturday afternoon with me because Aunt Shana was at the ice-cream parlor and when I told him I was going to cook dinner, he let me. He even went to the store and left me by myself. I don't need a babysitter anymore.

When he got back, he said Aunt Shana was upset with him for leaving me all alone, but nothing happened. I made macaroni and cheese in the microwave and baked Tater Tots and made a salad. It turned out really good, and guess what?

Uncle Adam and Aunt Shana kissed again, and they didn't even care that I could see them. I pretended I didn't, but I really did. They said they wanted to wash the dishes and it took them more than an hour. Miss you bunches and bunches.

Love,
Jazmine

Chapter Fourteen

If Ali had been at home instead of aboard the *USS Woodrow Wilson,* she would've turned to her favorite comfort food: cookie dough. It was that kind of day. Yes, she knew she shouldn't eat raw eggs. But when she reached this point—of being prepared to scarf down a bowl of unbaked cookies—salmonella seemed the least of her worries. Those ice-cream manufacturers knew what they were doing when they introduced cookie dough as a flavor. That, in her opinion, was the ultimate comfort food.

What had upset Ali, or rather *who,* was none other than Commander Frank Dillon. After managing fairly successfully to keep him out of her thoughts, he was back—not only in her thoughts, but unfortunately, in sick bay.

Earlier in the day he'd returned with a raging fever and an infection. Infection was the biggest risk with a ruptured appendix, and he hadn't been spared this complication. Ali was worried when she saw that his temperature was nearly 103 degrees. Furious, she'd asked why he hadn't come in earlier.

He'd refused to answer, but insisted that all he needed was a shot, and that once she'd given it to him, he could go back to his duties as navigator. When she told him Captain Coleman had ordered antibiotics via IV, he seemed to blame her personally. In his anger and frustration, he'd lashed out at her once again and questioned her competence.

As soon as he was hooked up to the antibiotics, and relatively free of pain, he slept for the remainder of her shift. Before leaving, she'd checked on him, taking his temperature, which had fallen to just over 100 degrees.

She felt both irritated and sad. Irritated that he'd delayed seeking medical attention. And sad because she suspected she might be the reason he'd stayed away. According to his own comments, he wanted nothing to do with her. She couldn't help wondering if that was because of her wedding ring—and yet how could it be? She'd removed it from her left hand.

Anytime he'd so much as glanced in her direction this afternoon, he'd scowled as if he couldn't bear to be in the same room. That was ridiculous. Ali hadn't done anything to deserve this wrath. After all, he was the one who'd sent her an e-mail thanking her for the excellent care. But from the way he regarded her now, anyone might think she'd attempted to amputate his leg while he wasn't looking. She tried not to dwell on the things he'd said to her, either today or during his first hospitalization, but she couldn't help that her feelings were hurt. She'd misread the situation and now he was back and not happy about it, either.

Frank didn't understand or recognize how serious this infection was. With a fever that high, he must've been terribly sick. Damn, he should never have waited this long!

Sent: July 7
From: Alison.Karas@woodrowwilson.navy.mil
To: Shana@mindsprung.com
Subject: It's cookie time!!

Dear Shana,

I'm tired and I want to come home. I sound like a crybaby but I don't care. The day has been long and awful, and if I was home right now I'd have the mixer going, blending sugar and flour and eggs with oatmeal and raisins. Yup, it's one of those days.

How are things with Jazmine? I need some news to cheer me up. Got anything wonderful to tell me? How's Adam? Any news about the transfer?

Love,
Alison

It wasn't long before she received a reply.

Sent: July 9
From: Shana@mindsprung.com
To: Alison.Karas@woodrowwilson.navy.mil
Subject: Fireworks and all

Dear Alison,

My goodness, what's happening? I haven't heard you sound so down in ages. When you start talking about cookie dough, I know there's got to be a man involved. I figure this must have something to do with that commander you mentioned. I thought you said you wouldn't be seeing him again. But apparently you have and it didn't go well. Tell all!

Jazmine is fabulous, but the truth is, I had a miserable day myself. I worked from dawn to dusk, and financially it was my best business day ever, so I should be happy, right? I wasn't. I wanted to be with Jazmine and Adam, who were off at a community fair while I was stuck at the ice-cream parlor.

I can't even begin to tell you how much work is involved in owning a business like this. Catherine was the only employee willing to work this weekend and thankfully, her husband came in to lend a hand. I don't know what I would've done otherwise. I *really* hated not being with Adam and Jazmine. They must've known it, because they showed up to collect me the minute I closed for the night. I didn't have time to change my clothes or anything. Adam drove to a hilltop where we had a picnic, even though it was almost dark. Adam had bought deli sandwiches and salads. By the time we arrived home, it was after eleven. I'm afraid I was exhausted and not much fun. Sometimes I wonder if buying this business was the wisest choice, but it's too late to think about that now.

Write soon.

Love,
Shana

Alison read her sister's e-mail and tried to translate the message between the lines. Like Alison, Shana was tired. According to Jazmine, she worked long hours, starting early in the morning when she mixed the pizza dough and set it out to rise. She usually stayed until closing, which meant she often wasn't home until after nine. Thankfully her sister had had the wherewithal to hire Catherine, who'd quickly become indispensable. Her other employees, mostly high-school kids, didn't seem all that reliable, but at least she had them.

Adam was spending a lot of time with Jazmine, and Alison knew very well that her daughter wasn't the only draw. He and Shana were definitely getting along, and that thrilled her. But if Adam was transferred to Hawaii, that might be the end of their relationship. Still, Alison couldn't worry about that when she had troubles of her own.

Fortunately, she had Lieutenant Rowland to talk to. He was waiting for her when she reported for duty the next afternoon.

"How's the beast doing?" she asked in a stage whisper. Compared to the commander, their other patients were downright jovial.

Jordan's responding grimace answered her question. "Same. Bad-tempered as ever."

"Oh, great."

Rowland rolled his eyes. "He's certainly got a burr under his saddle—and I think I know why."

Alison did, too. "He hates being sick." No one enjoyed it, but the commander was worse than most. He resented every minute away from his duty station. What he didn't realize was that he wouldn't be released anytime soon. She wasn't going to be the one to tell him, either.

"His problem," Rowland said with an air of superiority, "appears to be you."

"Me?" she protested, flustered that Frank's ranting from the day before had obviously continued.

"He asked me to keep you away from him."

Alison's face burned with mortification. "What did you tell him?" she asked, her voice indignant despite her efforts.

Rowland's smile lacked humor. "That the United States Navy was fortunate to have you, and if he has a problem he should take it up with Captain Coleman."

"Thank you," she said, and swallowed a painful knot of gratitude.

"The mighty commander didn't have anything to say after that."

"Good." Her anger simmering just below the surface, Alison squared her shoulders. "I think it's time I faced the beast on my own."

Rowland's dark eyes flared. "I don't know if I'd advise that."

Alison was past accepting her friend's advice. If Frank Dillon had even a clue what she was thinking, she'd likely be up for court-martial.

Before common sense and what remained of her Navy career could stop her, she tore back the curtain to his cubicle and confronted the commander. Although he appeared to be sleeping, he must have heard her because his eyes fluttered open.

"I understand you requested not to be under my care."

He blinked, and Alison was shocked to see that he refused to look at her. "You heard right."

"That's fine with me, Commander. As far as I'm concerned, you're cantankerous and impatient and rude and…and *more*."

Barely controlled anger showed in the tight set of his mouth. No one with any desire to advance in the Navy spoke to a senior officer the way Alison just had.

"What's the matter, Commander, no comment?" Feet braced apart, she gave him a defiant glare.

"It would be best if you left now," he muttered.

"I don't think so."

He frowned as if he'd rarely been challenged, but Alison was beyond caring.

"You don't like me, Commander, and that's perfectly okay, but I would prefer to keep personalities out of this. I am a professional and I pride myself on my work. Not only have you insulted me but you've—" Angry though she was, she couldn't complete the thought.

His eyes hardened, but he still wouldn't look at her.

Unable to bear another minute in his presence, she turned and walked away, feeling as though there was a huge hole in her stomach.

Chapter Fifteen

Shana was in much better spirits the following weekend. Her business continued to prosper, and she'd hired a new part-time employee, a teenage boy this time, named Charles. Not Charlie, but Charles. Hiring, training and dealing with employees had proved to be her biggest difficulty to date. This was an area where she had little experience and it seemed her lessons were all learned the hard way. She'd had to let the other two go and seemed to feel worse about it than either teenager. Charles was proving himself to be responsible and good-natured, and he and Catherine liked each other, quickly developing a bantering relationship. Shana couldn't even begin to imagine what she'd do without Catherine.

After several weeks of hanging around the ice-cream parlor, Jazmine's entrepreneurial talent suddenly kicked in, and her ideas weren't bad. The kid had real imagination when it came to inventing sundaes and candy treats. She took long strands of red and black licorice and—hands carefully gloved—braided them, decorating each end with colorful ribbons. Then she enclosed the entire creation in cellophane wrap. She hung them everywhere she found space, creating a festive atmosphere. The price was reasonable and the kids who came into the parlor were intrigued by them, so they sold quickly.

Jazmine's creativity had sparked Shana's, and she made up and displayed small bouquets using colorful lollipops and ribbons. The candy business contributed only a small portion to the total revenue but was gaining in popularity.

Working long hours had one advantage, Shana decided; she didn't have time to think about Adam's leaving. She was afraid it would be soon, and if she allowed herself to brood on it, she'd remember how much she enjoyed his company—and how much she was going to miss him.

Adam still hadn't mentioned the possibility of a transfer to Jazmine. Shana didn't feel it was her place to tell Jazz, unless Adam wanted her to, but he agreed the news should come from him. He'd promised he would last weekend, but then for one reason or another, he hadn't. Shana knew it would be hard to tell her and that he wanted to delay it until the transfer was official. She supposed it would be best to say nothing until he was sure. Her heart ached at the thought of Adam moving to Hawaii. Yes, it was a wonderful assignment and one he'd sought out, but Shana wanted him in Seattle, selfish though that was...

At the height of the lunch business, when the restaurant smelled of baking dough and tomato sauce, and it was all Shana could do to keep up with the pizza orders, the phone rang. Catherine bustled over to answer it and her gaze flew to Shana.

"It's for you," she said, holding out the receiver.

Shana finished slicing a sausage pizza still steaming hot from the oven. If it was Adam, she'd call back the minute she had time to breathe. "Who is it?" she asked.

"Adam, I think," Catherine told her.

She realized he might have news; if so, she wanted to know as soon as possible. "Ask him if it's important."

Catherine grabbed the phone and as Shana watched, the older woman nodded at her.

Her stomach tensed with anxiety. Shana could feel it coming even before he told her. Adam had received his transfer papers or whatever the Navy called them. That must be it; otherwise he would've phoned her tonight.

Wiping her hands on her apron, she asked Charles to fill in for her while she answered the phone. "Could you bring this pizza to table ten?"

"Sure."

Shana walked to the other side of the room and took the phone from Catherine. "Adam?"

"I'm sorry to bother you now."

She leaned against the wall, hardly able to breathe.

"Listen," he said, and she could hear the regret in his voice.

She could think of no reason to delay his news, so she said it before he had a chance. "You got the transfer to Hawaii."

"Yes, my orders hit the boards."

"They what?"

"They're official. And I have to fly out almost right away. The officer I'm replacing had an emergency."

There it was, what she'd dreaded most. "I see." Shana closed her eyes. Although she'd known this was coming, she still felt a sense of shock. The tightness in her chest was painful, and she bit her lower lip to keep from protesting aloud.

"I fly out in the morning."

"So soon?" She'd hoped they'd have some time to say their farewells. At least one more chance to talk and decide—not that there was really anything to decide. But it felt wrong for him to go like this, so quickly, without any opportunity for Jazmine or her to adjust.

"I'm sorry," he said.

"I know." She couldn't seem to say more than two words at a time. "Tonight?" she managed through her painfully dry throat.

Despite her lack of clarity or detail, he understood the question. "Unfortunately, I can't. There's too much to do."

"I know…"

"Is Jazmine there?"

Shana pressed her hand against her forehead. "No, she's at the park skating with her friends."

"You may need to tell her for me."

"No!" Shana's objection was immediate. "You *have* to do it."

"I'll phone if I can, but there are no guarantees. She's a Navy kid. She'll understand."

Until recently Shana hadn't had much to do with the Navy. All at once she found her entire life affected by it, and frankly she was starting to get annoyed.

"I'll be in touch, I promise," Adam assured her. "Leaving you and Jazmine like this isn't what I want, either."

His words didn't lessen the dejection she felt. She remembered, in an immediate and visceral way, the emotions she'd experienced when she saw Brad and Sylvia together, knowing exactly what they were doing. The sensation that she'd lost something vital had refused to go away. With Brad that was the signal she'd needed, because what they'd had wasn't real, not on his part, anyway. With Adam...with Adam all she felt was loss.

"I don't want you to go." She knew it was childish to say that.

"I'll be able to visit. About Jazz—I've got meetings this afternoon, and tonight I have to pack. I'll phone when I can. *If* I can."

Shana knew what he was asking. She sighed wearily. "I'll tell her."

"I'm sorry to put this on you, but if I don't reach her, you'll have to."

"I know."

"I meant what I said," he reiterated. "I'll visit as often as I can."

While Adam might have every intention of flying in to see them, it would be time-consuming and complicated. Shana recalled that the flight between Hawaii and Portland was a good five hours. She'd taken a brief vacation there with friends; it was the longest flight she'd ever taken. Yes, his intentions were good but that was all they were—intentions.

"I've got your e-mail address," he reminded her. "Yours and Jazmine's, and I'll stay in touch."

"You promise?" She hated the fact that she still sounded like a thwarted child, but she couldn't pretend this wasn't hard.

"Yes—I promise."

Shana had no choice but to comfort herself with his word. Doing her best to seem reconciled to what was happening, she straightened. "Have a safe flight, and don't worry about Jazmine. I'll explain everything to her."

"Thank you."

"No…Adam, thank you." Her voice cracked before she finished and she knew she had to get off the phone or she'd embarrass herself further. "I'm sorry, but I really need to get back to work now."

"I understand, but Shana, one last thing—about you and me. We have to talk. Soon, okay?"

She didn't answer. She couldn't. Replacing the receiver, she let her hand linger while she struggled to overcome her disappointment. With Adam stationed in Hawaii, she could forecast their future and she didn't need the aid of a crystal ball. For Jazmine's sake, he'd stay in touch. Later, when Alison returned and Jazmine went back to live with her mother, he and Shana would both make an effort. At least in the beginning. Then their time together would dwindle until they were forced to face the inevitable. It was how long-distance relationships usually ended.

Shana had seen it with friends. Couples would e-mail back and forth, and on special occasions they'd phone, just for the pleasure of hearing each other's voices. Adam could fly on military transports, so there might even be a weekend now and then when he'd be able to visit the mainland, but she suspected those opportunities would be few and far between. They'd both try, but in the end the obstacles would be too much.

Adam had been a brief season in her life. Instead of complaining, she should be grateful. The lieutenant commander had given her back her self-confidence; he'd made her feel beautiful and...cherished. When she'd met him, another relationship was the last thing on her mind. But Adam had proved there were still good men left in this world, and that not every man was like Brad.

"Are you okay?" Catherine asked, joining her. She rested a gentle hand on Shana's shoulder. "Was it bad news?"

"Everything's all right," she said, shaking her head in order to dispel the lethargic feeling that had stolen over her. "Or it will be soon," she amended.

The look Catherine threw her said she wasn't convinced, and of course the older woman's instincts were accurate. Heaviness settled over Shana's heart. She didn't know why her relationships with men always fell apart. In retrospect, though, she realized she'd carried the relationship with Brad. She'd trusted, believed and held on. She refused to do that with Adam. She wanted a relationship of equals or not at all—and she'd grown increasingly sure that this was it. Her future. Good grief, she was reading a lot into a couple of kisses! It was just that everything had felt so right—and now this.

An hour later, just when the pizza sales had started to diminish, Jazmine returned, her face red and sweaty from her trek around Lincoln Park on her Rollerblades.

"I sold three more of your licorice braids," Shana told her, trying to act normal.

Jazmine shrugged, but Shana could tell she was pleased. Shana had managed to pick up quite a bit of the girl's body language. It wasn't cool to show too much enthusiasm if there was the slightest possibility someone her own age would see it.

As long as Shana remembered that, she was fine. But when she forgot, problems developed. However, if Jazmine and Shana were alone, or if it was Jazz with Shana and Adam, a completely different set of behavioral rules applied.

"Would you like to make up a few more?" Shana asked.

"Maybe."

This meant she'd be happy to, but not if a friend came by and thought she'd willingly agreed to do anything with or for an adult.

"Good."

At closing time, Shana counted out the money from the cash register, while Jazmine sat in a booth curled up with a book. Every now and then, Shana felt the girl's eyes on her. Catherine and Charles were finishing the cleanup in the kitchen.

"Is there anything I should know about?" her niece asked as soon as they were alone. She laid her book on the tabletop, her elbows on either side of it, and stared at Shana.

Jazmine's intuition surprised her. Shana stopped in midcount and looked up. "Like what?"

Jazmine frowned. "I'm not sure, but I have the feeling you know something I don't. I hate that."

Shana wrapped elastics around the bills of various denominations, setting each stack aside. "I always did, too," she said. After tucking the cash in the deposit bag, she joined her niece, sliding into the booth across from her.

"So there *is* something wrong." Jazmine's eyes seemed to grow darker. "My mom's okay, isn't she?" Her anxiety was unconcealed, and Shana wanted to reassure her as quickly as possible.

"Oh, yes! No worries there."

"Then what's wrong?"

Her sigh of relief touched Shana's heart. "This has to do with your uncle Adam." How times changed. Only recently she'd begrudged Adam the term *uncle*. At first, the word had nearly gotten stuck in her throat, but now it fell easily from her lips.

Shana was going to miss him so much, but at the moment she was furious that he'd left the job of telling Jazmine up to her—even if she'd agreed to it. "What about Uncle Adam?" Jazmine's eyes seemed more frightened by the second. She scrambled out of the booth.

Shana stood, too, and placed her arm around Jazmine's thin shoulders, but her niece shook it off. In her need to comfort the girl, Shana had forgotten the rules.

"Just *tell* me," Jazmine insisted.

Shana decided her niece was right. She'd give Jazmine the news as clearly, honestly and straightforwardly as she could. "The Navy is reassigning him to Hawaii."

Jazmine spent a moment digesting the information. This was followed by a series of quickly fired questions. "When's he flying out? He is flying, isn't he? Does he get leave first? Because he should. What about the garden? He said he'd help and isn't there a whole lot more that needs to be done? Besides, he promised me he'd be here and…and now he's breaking his word." As if she'd said too much she covered her mouth with both hands.

Shana didn't know how to respond, where to start. "He phoned this afternoon to say his orders, uh, hit the boards and he had to leave first thing in the morning."

Jazmine's eyes flared. "Already?" She sounded shocked, disbelieving.

"I'm afraid so."

"When did he find out?"

"He just got the final word this afternoon."

"But he must've known *something* before now."

Shana nodded.

"He never said a word."

"I know." Shana could kick him for that, especially now that she was the one telling Jazmine.

Jazmine sat down again and glared at Shana suspiciously. "He told you before this afternoon, though, didn't he?"

Shana could probably talk her way out of this, but she didn't want to lie to her niece. "He did, or…well, he mentioned the possibility. But he dreaded telling you, so he put it off. Besides, he wasn't sure it would go through at all and certainly not this soon."

"So he made you tell me." Jazmine's anger was unmistakable, despite the softness of her voice.

Shana nodded. Adam would pay dearly for that, she suspected.

Jazmine considered this information for a couple of minutes, then casually tossed back her hair. Propping her chin on her palm, she sat very still. "How do you feel about this?"

"I'm fine with it." Shana managed to sound almost flippant. "But to be on the safe side, I'm bringing home a container of chocolate-mint ice cream."

Her niece gave her a confused look.

"I'm throwing myself a pity party," Shana explained. "You're invited."

"What are we going to do other than eat ice cream?"

"Watch old movies," Shana decided. The two of them could snuggle up together in front of the television, wearing their oldest pajamas.

"*Sleepless in Seattle* is one of my mom's favorites," her niece told her. Apparently the kid was familiar with this particular brand of mood therapy. Shana would have to ask Alison about it at the first opportunity. Perhaps tonight, when she e-mailed her sister.

"Do you have any others we could watch?" Jazmine asked. "I've seen *Sleepless* so often I can say all the lines."

"The Bridges of Madison County," she suggested, but sometimes that one made her angry, when what she really wanted was to weep copiously at a fictional character's tragic life. Pure catharsis, in other words.

"Mom said I was too young to see it," Jazmine muttered disgustedly, as though she no longer required parental guidance.

At times it was hard to remember that her niece was only nine. The kid was mature beyond her years. Alison was right about the movie, though. A story featuring infidelity hardly seemed appropriate for a child.

"For her pity parties, Mom likes popcorn best. The more butter the better," she said matter-of-factly. "We had several of them after Dad died. But Mom didn't call them pity parties."

"What did she call them?"

"Tea parties, but we only had them when we were feeling sad."

"Always with buttered popcorn?"

"It goes good with tea," Jazmine said. "I don't think she had a name for them at first. I woke up one night and saw her crying in front of the TV, and she said sad movies always made her cry. Then I asked her why she watched them."

Shana already knew the answer to that. "Because she needed a good cry."

Jazmine nodded again. "That's exactly what Mom said." The girl sighed heavily, then added in a small voice, "I don't want her to be sad."

"Me, neither, but it's part of life, Jazz. It's not good to be *too* sad or for too long, but being sad has its place. For one thing, sadness makes happiness that much more wonderful."

Jazmine looked at her thoughtfully, awareness dawning in her eyes.

"Now, it's been a while since I had an official pity party," Shana said briskly. "One is long overdue." She'd made a couple of weak attempts when she left Brad, but she'd been too angry with him to do it properly. If anything, their breakup had left her feeling strong and decisive. That high hadn't lasted, and she'd found it emotionally difficult to reconcile herself to the end of the relationship—but only for a short time. Thanks to Adam…

She thought that breaking off her engagement—or whatever it was—with Brad did call for a party, but a real party with banners and food, champagne and music and lots of people. She smiled as she considered how far she'd come.

"What's so funny?" Jazmine asked.

Shana instantly sobered. "Remember a few weeks ago, when you said I had issues?"

"Yeah."

"One of those issues was Brad."

Jazmine rolled her eyes. "Tell me about it!"

Shana laughed out loud. "I was just thinking I never really had a pity party over him."

Jazmine cocked her head quizzically. "Do women always throw these parties because of men?"

"Hmm."

Shana had never given the matter much thought. "Yes," she said firmly. "It's always about men."

"That's what I figured." Jazmine shook her head sadly, as if this reasoning was beyond her.

They loaded up with chocolate-mint ice cream, and whipped topping for good measure, and headed out the door. Shana had to make a quick stop at the bank, but they were home before the ice cream had a chance to melt.

Within ten minutes, they were both lying on their backs, dressed in old flannel pajamas, studying the ceiling.

"Remember when Brad phoned you a little while ago?" Jazmine asked.

"Yup." Shana didn't want to dwell on Brad. She wanted to think about Adam and how much they were going to miss him. Brad paled in comparison to Adam Kennedy.

"Why did he call?"

Shana rolled onto her stomach and raised her head. "He realized the error of his ways."

Jazmine rolled over, too. "Are you going to take him back?"

Shana didn't even need to think about it. "No."

Jazmine solemnly agreed. "He had his turn."

Boy, did he!

"Uncle Adam is next in line."

It occurred to Shana to explain that pity parties were usually wakes for relationships. This wake was for Adam and her. Shana was cutting her losses now, doing her best to accept the likely end of their brief romance and move forward.

"What if Brad came to Seattle?" Jazmine asked excitedly, as if that were a distinct possibility. "What would you do then?"

Shana flopped onto her back again. "Nothing."

"Not a thing?"

"Not a single, solitary thing."

"What if he offered you an engagement ring?"

Shana grinned. "First, I'd faint from the shock of it, and then I'd...I'd ask to see his ID. Make sure this was really Brad."

"Would you cry?"

"I doubt it."

"But you'd turn him down, right?"

"Wait a minute." Shana pulled herself into a sitting position. "Is there any particular reason for all these questions about Brad?"

Jazmine sighed loudly. "I wanted to be sure you're really, really over that rat."

"Rat?"

"That's what Mom called him."

Shana smothered a giggle. "Hey, I thought we were throwing this party because of your uncle Adam," she said. It hadn't escaped her notice how cleverly Jazmine had changed the subject.

"We are."

"So, why bring up Brad?"

Her question was met with silence, and then Jazmine ventured, "Remember how you knew Uncle Adam might be stationed in Hawaii and you didn't tell me?"

"Yes, but what's that got to do with—" She hesitated and drew in her breath. "Is there something *you* aren't telling *me?*" she demanded, aware that she was repeating Jazmine's earlier question.

Her niece sighed dramatically. "Promise you won't be mad."

"Jazmine!"

"Okay, okay. Brad phoned again. I answered and I told him you're seeing someone else now."

"You didn't!"

Jazmine giggled. "I did, and you don't want to know what he said about that, either."

Chapter Sixteen

"What do you mean Brad phoned?" Shana demanded. "When? And why?" Not that she cared. Okay, she did, but only a little. He'd talked to her once, a few weeks ago, and she'd been polite and stiff and frankly had never expected to hear from him again. At one time, she'd dreamed about a big wedding with lots of bridesmaids all dressed in lovely pastel dresses of pink and yellow. Her sister and three of her best friends would've looked like a neat row of huge after-dinner mints. At least she'd spared them that.

"He called last week and I answered the phone," Jazmine muttered. "We…talked. For a while."

That sounded ominous. Shana could only imagine what Brad had to say to her niece—and vice versa.

"He told me he wants you back."

"Of course he does," Shana muttered. *That* made

sense. Now that she was out of his life, he missed everything she'd done for him.

"When he asked how your social life was these days—that's exactly what he said—I told him about Uncle Adam and he wasn't very happy," Jazmine continued.

"No," Shana agreed. "He probably wasn't." Just like Brad to pump a nine-year-old for information.

"I shouldn't have said anything," Jazmine muttered, "but I wanted Brad to know he lost out on the opportunity of a lifetime."

That was a typically grandiose Jazmine remark, and Shana smiled. Still, it was gratifying to know Brad missed her, even if it was for the wrong reasons. He must've been shocked to learn she'd met someone else.

"I hope you aren't mad."

"No, but…it isn't a good idea to be giving out personal information over the phone."

"I know, but he kept asking me about your social life and if you were seeing anyone, and it felt good to tell him you were and that Uncle Adam is a lieutenant commander in the United States Navy." This was said with a good deal of pride.

Shana bet that caused ol' Brad to sit up and take notice.

"I wish my mom was here," Jazmine confessed suddenly. "I'm worried about her."

Shana wrapped her arm around Jazmine's shoulders and drew her close. "She seems to be in good spirits." Or she had been until recently.

"She sounds happy when she e-mails me," Jazmine said. "But sometimes I wonder if she's telling the truth."

The kid certainly had her mother pegged.

Jazmine leaned against Shana. "This has been good,"

she said decisively. "It's even better than a tea party. Except we didn't watch a movie or eat our ice cream—but we can do that now. How about…the first Harry Potter movie? I've got the DVD."

"Sure."

"I'm going to miss Uncle Adam," Jazmine told her sadly. "It won't be the same without him."

Shana could only agree.

Jazmine was asleep an hour later. She lay curled up on the sofa with an afghan covering her. Shana turned off the television set and logged on to the computer.

Sent: July 15
From: Shana@mindsprung.com
To: Alison.Karas@woodrowwilson.navy.mil
Subject: My love/hate relationship with men!

Dear Ali,

I hope you realize what a terrific kid you have. Jazmine and I have just spent the last two hours sharing secrets (plus eating ice cream and watching a Harry Potter movie).

Adam got his orders for Hawaii and didn't even have time to say goodbye. Even worse, I got stuck telling Jazmine.

Trust me, I wasn't too happy with him. I would've let him know how I felt about that, but I was in shock. Do transfers always happen this fast in the Navy? Never mind, he already explained that they don't.

Getting back to Jazmine. She took the news about Adam fairly well. I wasn't sure what I expected and I know she's upset, but as Adam said, she's a Navy kid. She did ask if I knew in advance, and I had to confess that I did. Once I admitted I'd been holding out on her, her own heavily guarded secret came out.

Are you ready for this? Our Jazmine had a conversation with Brad! Apparently he phoned and she informed him I was seeing someone else. I wish she hadn't…. Well, to be honest, that's not entirely true. He told Jazmine that he misses me. Interesting, don't you think? Not to worry, I'd never go back to him.

Once we'd both confessed our secrets, we talked about you and discovered we're both concerned. Jazz is afraid you're hiding your feelings from her—and Alison, I have to tell you that your daughter has good instincts. I didn't say anything, but I know you've been down lately. You refuse to answer my questions about Commander Dillon, and my guess is this involves him. I know, I know, you've already said it a dozen times—there's nothing between you. Technically I'm sure that's true, but…there's more to the situation, isn't there?

What you say or don't say to Jazz is up to you, but she sees through you far too easily, so don't try to pull the wool over her eyes. Jazmine would rather deal with the truth than worry about what's troubling you.

Oh, one last thing. The kid has graduated from tea parties to ice cream. You can thank me for that.

Keep in touch.

Love,
Shana

The following evening, when Shana arrived home from work exhausted, cranky and hungry for something other than pizza or canned chili, the phone rang. With unwarranted optimism, she opened the refrigerator and searched for inspiration—something easy and fast that would pass for healthy. Or sort of healthy. The wilted green pepper, leftover Chinese fried rice and half can of clam chowder weren't appealing.

The phone was still ringing and Shana looked around to see where Jazmine had disappeared. Normally she didn't need to worry about answering the phone because her niece leaped on it like a hungry cat on a cornered mouse.

"I'll get it," she called out when she saw that the bathroom door was closed. Grabbing the phone, Shana cradled it against her shoulder and turned to the cupboard in a second attempt to find a supper solution.

"Hello." The cupboard, stacked with canned foods, offered little in the way of ideas.

"Shana."

"Adam?" In her excitement she nearly dropped the phone. She'd hoped she'd hear from him, but hadn't dared believe. He missed her, he said; he'd been thinking about her. Instantly her heart went on alert. She was afraid to put too much weight on a single phone call and yet so pleased it was all she could do not to leap up and down.

"How's my girl?" he asked in a low, sexy voice.

Shana sighed and leaned against the wall. "I'm doing great." Especially now that she'd heard from him.

"I was asking about Jazmine," he teased.

Shana laughed. "She's great, too. I want you to know we had a pity party over you."

"A what?"

"Never mind—it's a girl thing." She felt so buoyant, so happy, she couldn't prevent a giggle from slipping out.

Adam went directly to the reason for his call. "I got an e-mail from Jazmine and it started me thinking."

"You received an e-mail from her already?"

"Actually she sent this before I flew out. Can I ask you something?"

"Sure."

"Jazz said that Brad phoned you recently."

"Jealous?" she asked lightly, dismissing the question because he had no reason for concern. It would be manipulative to play one man against another, and she refused to do it.

"A little," he admitted with obvious reluctance. "I need to know if you're serious about Brad."

"You're phoning me all the way from Hawaii because you're afraid of a little competition?" she asked. "Adam, you should know better than that."

"Competition doesn't frighten me, but I have to know where I stand with you."

"I can't believe you're talking about Brad," she said, letting her bewilderment show in her voice.

Adam held his ground. "According to Jazmine, you

have what she calls *issues* and one of those issues is Brad, and I figured—"

"Brad," she interrupted, "is out of my life."

"Apparently no one bothered to tell him that. I know of two times he's contacted you. Are there others?"

Shana was completely dumbfounded now. "You men are all alike," she snapped. "You're so…so territorial. Why are we even having this conversation?" She lifted the hair from her forehead and pressed her hand there as if to contain her outrage—or her growing headache. Unfortunately it didn't work. She could think of only one reason Brad had revealed any new interest, and that was because he believed she'd become involved with another man. He considered Shana "his." Now Adam was doing the very same thing.

"Are you upset with me?" he had the audacity to ask.

"You must be joking." If she had to tell him, then there was something lacking in her communication skills. "Yes, Adam, I am upset. You don't seem to care about *me*. Your big concern is that I might be tempted to go back to Brad."

They both took a moment to let the sparks die down. Shana was afraid to say anything more, afraid the conversation would deteriorate further and they'd reach a point of no return.

The bathroom door opened then and Jazmine stepped out, hair wrapped in a towel.

"Here," Shana said, shoving the telephone receiver toward her. "It's your uncle Adam. Talk to him."

"Shana, we aren't finished yet," she heard him yell.

"Oh, yes, we are," she said loud and clear. She just couldn't resist.

Jazmine tentatively accepted the phone, but the conversation was short. Angry, and uncertain how to cope with her anger, Shana paced across the kitchen floor to the window and stood there, staring out at the garden.

Jazmine turned to her after she'd hung up the phone. "Should I get out the ice cream?"

Shana managed to smile. "You know, that doesn't sound like a bad idea."

Chapter Seventeen

Commander Frank Dillon figured he had to be the biggest jerk alive, but in his own defense, his behavior toward SMO Karas was motivated strictly by self-preservation.

A week after he'd gone back to sick bay, he was released. Unfortunately, it wasn't soon enough. Every second he spent in close proximity to Alison was pure agony. More times than he wanted to admit, he had to remind himself that she was married. Married with a capital *M*. All he had to do was glance at the ring to remember she was off-limits. Granted, she'd switched it to her right hand, but that act of deception actually bothered him more.

He'd fallen for her, and fallen hard. Whenever he saw her, his heart did a free fall—like a paratrooper diving from a plane—until he saw that damned ring. Then he knew it was time to pull the rip cord and put an end to his ridiculous fascination with the woman.

This sort of thing didn't happen. Not to him. He was particularly confused by the fact that although Alison wore a wedding band, she'd sent him some pretty clear signals—signals that said she was interested and available. While he was undeniably tempted, Frank felt sickened by her lack of respect for her husband and her vows. He wanted nothing more to do with her.

Back on the bridge at the end of his shift, Frank knew the crew had been eagerly waiting for the *USS Woodrow Wilson* to make its port call in Guam. Shore leave had been granted.

During his years in the Navy, Frank had sailed all over the world, and his favorite destination was the South Pacific. He'd read many accounts of the action here during World War II, as well as histories of the explorers.

"You headed ashore?" Commander Howden asked, joining Frank on the bridge.

Frank, still feeling the effects of his surgery, had decided against leaving the carrier. There would be ample opportunity on other voyages. "Not this time."

"A few of us are talking about golf and dinner. Why don't you come along?"

"Thanks, I'll give it some thought." Frank wouldn't willingly admit it, but he felt too weak. A round of golf would probably do him in.

Howden started to walk away, then unexpectedly turned back. "I met the senior medical officer the other day—Alison Karas," he said casually.

Frank stiffened at the sound of her name.

"She's a good woman. I knew her husband."

Frank's jaw tightened at his use of the past tense. "Knew?"

Hal nodded. "He was killed a couple of years ago in a training accident. He'd been aboard the *USS Abraham Lincoln*. You heard about it," he said.

"Yes—but I didn't make the connection." Frank spoke quietly.

"No reason you should, I suppose," Howden continued. "I just realized it myself."

Frank felt angry with himself for the false assumptions he'd made. Alison was a widow and all along, all this time, he'd believed she was married and unfaithful. He hated everything he'd been thinking about her, hated the way he'd magnified her supposed transgressions in his mind. He knew why he'd done it—because he was afraid of what might happen.

As soon as possible, Frank went down to sick bay. He needed—no, wanted—to apologize. He couldn't explain his behavior, but he could let Alison know he regretted what he'd said and done. Perhaps the best course of action was to leave things as they were, but he was unwilling to do that.

He found Lieutenant Rowland on duty in sick bay. Not an enviable task when the majority of his shipmates were touring paradise. The lieutenant snapped to attention when Frank came in.

"Can I help you, Commander?"

Frank returned the salute. "At ease. I'm looking for Ali. Do you know where I might find her?"

"Ali?" The young officer couldn't hide his surprise. "I'm sorry, sir, she's gone ashore."

Frank had guessed as much. "Did she happen to mention where she was going?"

"No, sir, but I suspect she's headed toward the Farmer's Market. A few of the other women officers mentioned they were planning to check it out."

"Thank you," Frank said as he spun around. His energy had been waning, but adrenaline pumped through him now as he hurried off the ship. Fortunately, he was familiar with the island and grabbed the first taxi he saw, paying the driver handsomely.

The streets swarmed with sailors, tourists and locals. The carnival-like atmosphere was everywhere. Music played, chickens squawked and locals hawked their wares, eager to separate the sailors from their hard-earned dollars. The market was so crowded it was nearly impassable.

In this mass of humanity, Frank wondered if locating Alison was a lost cause. That didn't discourage him, but he knew his odds weren't good.

What he should do, Frank decided after a fruitless hour, was think like a woman. The problem with that was he didn't *know* how a woman thought. If he did, his marriage might've lasted longer than two years.

Marriage. The word shot through his brain. Even if he located Ali, he wasn't sure exactly what he'd say to her, or how she'd react. He'd apologize, that much he knew. He must've been intolerable the entire time he was in sick bay, and he admired the way she'd confronted him, admired her professionalism. It wasn't easy to admit he'd been a colossal jerk; if for no other reason, Frank owed her an apology. Then, with his conscience clear, he'd walk away and that would be the end of it.

Suddenly he saw her. She was with a group of female officers, examining a bolt of silk. A flower lei was draped around her neck and the sun shone on her gleaming dark hair. Gazing at her, Frank stood stock-still as the human traffic moved around him.

He watched Ali run her palm over the red silk and ask the proprietor one question and then another. Frank couldn't hear the man's response, but apparently she didn't like it because she promptly shook her head and left without further haggling.

She hadn't seen Frank, since she was moving straight toward him. He remained frozen, waiting for her to notice that he was there. The two women with her recognized him first. One of them, another lieutenant commander, tilted her head toward Alison and he saw Alison's eyes swing in his direction. Almost immediately she looked away, an expression of discomfort on her face.

"Lieutenant Commander Karas," he said crisply, stepping up to her. Perhaps she'd think he was on official business. "I need a moment of your time."

She blinked as if gathering her composure.

He scowled at her companions and they quickly took the hint.

"We'll meet up with you later," one friend stated, setting off.

The other lingered a moment, obviously concerned about leaving Ali in the company of the ogre patient. But at Ali's nod, she rejoined the first woman.

"How can I help you, Commander?" Ali asked. Her shoulders were back as if she expected another ugly confrontation.

Frank wasn't good at apologizing. It wasn't something he'd had much practice at. He began to speak, and then paused to clear his throat before he could get out even one short sentence. "I want to apologize for last week."

Her eyes flared briefly, but she didn't respond.

"I have no excuse for my rude and arrogant behavior," he went on, repeating the very words she'd used to describe him. He despised humiliation in any form, but in this instance he deserved it.

"Apology accepted, Commander. No one likes being sick and helpless."

"That's true," he agreed, willing to accept her explanation.

His remark was followed by silence. Frank usually didn't have problems expressing his views, but just then, standing in a crowded market in the middle of a South Pacific island—standing there with Ali—he couldn't think of a single intelligent thing to say.

"I appreciate everything you did to make my stay as comfortable as possible," he muttered.

"You're welcome," she said abruptly. She seemed eager to leave.

Frank didn't blame her.

"Is there anything else?" she prodded when he didn't resume the conversation.

"No," he said without inflection, but he wanted to scream that there *was.* He just didn't know how to say it. Had they been anyplace else, he might have found the courage to let her know he admired her.

Without another word, she turned and walked toward her friends who stood at a booth, ignoring the proprietor and focusing their attention on him and Ali. Both women seemed to have plenty of opinions, because their heads were close together and they talked rapidly. Frank hated being the object of their scrutiny, but there was no help for it. He'd done what he could; now he had to leave things as they were.

"Lieutenant Commander Karas," he called out sharply, stopping her.

Alison glanced over her shoulder.

"I heard—I'm sorry about your husband."

For the briefest of moments, in the second or two it took her to blink, Alison's eyes went liquid with grief. She quickly regained control of her emotions. "Thank you, Commander. Like you, Peter dedicated his life to the Navy."

He nodded and felt properly put in his place.

That said, Ali joined her friends. The three of them left and were swallowed up by the crowd.

If searching for Ali was out of character, what he did next was even more so. He returned to the silk merchant and purchased the entire bolt of fabric Alison had so recently examined. The hell if he knew what to do with fifteen yards of red silk.

Chapter Eighteen

"I'd like to talk to you when you've got a free moment," Catherine said as soon as Shana showed up for work Monday morning.

Dread instantly filled her. It was said bad news came in threes. Adam had left for Hawaii, Brad wanted her back—or so he'd claimed—and now she feared the worst calamity of all. Her most valued employee was about to quit. Shana could deal with just about anything except that.

"N-now is convenient," she managed to stutter. It wasn't, but she'd have an ulcer if she put this off.

Catherine joined her in the kitchen but kept an eye on the ice-cream counter in case a customer came in.

"You aren't going to quit, are you?" Shana asked point-blank. Catherine had quickly become her friend and confidante. "Because if you do, I'm throwing in the towel right now."

Catherine brushed aside her concern with a wave of her hand. "Of course I'm not quitting. I love my job."

Relief washed over her, and Shana reached out to hug the other woman. "I'm so grateful… I don't think I could take much more."

"That's one of the reasons I thought we should talk," Catherine said. "I don't mean to put my nose where it doesn't belong, but like I said when you interviewed me, I worked in the school cafeteria for almost fifteen years. We were a close-knit group and were able to discuss everything with one another."

"I want you to feel free to do the same here," Shana assured her.

A smile relaxed the older woman's features, and Shana could see that she'd been worried. "Okay. I have a couple of ideas I'd like to try out, so we can take ice-cream requests in a more orderly fashion," Catherine said, "but I understand this is your business and I won't take offense if you don't think they'll work."

"Anything you can suggest would be appreciated," Shana told her. "You're my most important asset, and I want you to know that."

"I wrote everything out for you to read at your leisure," Catherine said, handing her an envelope.

Shana tucked it inside her apron pocket. "Please feel free to share any ideas you have with me," she said. "I'm interested in all your suggestions."

Catherine positively beamed at the praise. "Now, I don't want you to get the notion that I'm taking over the shop or being dictatorial," she said.

That notion was laughable. "I'd never have survived the last couple of weekends without you and your husband."

Catherine's eyes brightened at the mention of her husband. "Louis had the time of his life."

They'd been wonderful with the customers and reminded Shana of the Olsens, who'd owned the shop for all those years. Catherine and Louis were so natural with children and treated everyone like family. Shana envied their ability, and knew this kind of friendliness was a big reason her customers returned over and over again. She'd been fortunate to hire Catherine, and Louis was a bonus...and a darling.

"You know who to call if you want another day off." Catherine smiled. "In fact, Louis said if you're ever looking to sell, we'd like the right of first refusal, but I told him you'd just bought the business and it wasn't likely you'd be interested in selling."

"No, but I'll certainly keep that in mind." Shana had invested her entire financial future in this shop. So far, she was meeting payroll and keeping her head above water, but this was her busy season. The Olsens had warned her that the winter months could be a fiscal challenge. Shana hoped to find ways to stay afloat when the weather was dreary. Ice-cream sales would decrease in winter, but she hoped the pizza part of the business would continue to flourish. Thankfully, Lincoln Park was much-used year round.

"Also," Catherine added, sounding hesitant. "I know this isn't any of my concern, but it seems to me you haven't been yourself the last few days."

So it was that obvious.

"Is there a problem?" the other woman asked gently, in the same way Ali might have done had she been there. Trading e-mails was better than nothing but they weren't a substitute for face-to-face communication.

Shana slumped against the wall and automatically shook her head. For three nights straight, she hadn't slept more than a couple of hours. When she did manage to drift off, she dreamed of Adam and then woke tired and depressed.

"Man troubles?" Catherine asked. "You don't need to tell me, not unless you want. But sometimes just talking things out with someone else can help."

Shana nodded, reflecting that the school district had lost a wonderful employee. In Shana's opinion, Catherine was much too young to retire.

"It's just that, well…this is complicated." Shana wasn't sure how to explain without going into more detail than necessary.

"Does this have to do with Brad or Adam?" Catherine prompted.

Shana's mouth fell open. "How do you know about Brad?" Her eyes narrowed and she answered her own question. It could only be her niece. "Jazmine."

Catherine nodded, folding her hands. She looked about as guilty as a woman can. "Jazmine and I are friends, and the truth of it is, she confided in me because she's worried about you."

"She is, is she?" Shana couldn't wait to ask Jazmine about this.

"Jazmine is a dear girl and she meant well," Catherine said immediately.

"Who else has she told?" Shana demanded. Apparently her heart-to-heart with her niece hadn't been as effective as she'd hoped. Jazmine seemed intent on spreading Shana's problems throughout the entire neighborhood.

"I don't think she's mentioned it to anyone else,"

Catherine was quick to reassure her. "Certainly not Charles. I can't be positive, of course, but…" Her voice trailed off.

"Of course," Shana echoed. Jazmine was a handful. Spending her days at the park with friends or in the ice-cream parlor with Shana wasn't the ideal situation, but it was the best that could be done for now. Unless Shana looked into some kind of summer camp for her…

"The only reason Jazmine said anything was because I asked her if she knew what was bothering you. So if anyone's to blame, it's me," Catherine insisted, her face reddening. "I apologize, Shana."

"Don't worry about it." But Shana decided she'd still ask Jazmine later.

"Is there anything I can do to help?" Catherine offered. "Like I said, I'm a good listener."

After several sleepless nights, Shana could use some advice. "All right," she agreed with a deep sigh. "My life's a bit of a mess at the moment," she said, then proceeded to tell Catherine about her five-year relationship with Brad and how it had ended. She described how he'd been an important part of her life, and then he was gone; just after that, Jazmine had arrived and on the heels of her niece Adam Kennedy showed up.

Catherine nodded often during the course of their lengthy one-sided discussion.

"Are you in love with Adam?" she asked when Shana had finished.

"Yes. *No.* How can I be?" She paused. "Good grief, I'm the last person who'd know."

"You love Brad, though?" Catherine continued.

"No." This came without the slightest hesitation. "Although I loved him at one time. At least, I believed I did."

"I don't think breaking off a relationship is ever as easy as we want it to be," Catherine said thoughtfully. "We invest our hopes and dreams in a particular relationship, and when that doesn't work out, we sometimes have difficulty admitting it."

"That's true." Shana nodded, remembering the years she'd devoted to Brad with such hope for a future together.

"I wonder if what you really want is for Brad to recognize how much he wronged you."

Shana grinned. That was so true, it was almost painful.

"It gives women a sense of vindication," Catherine pronounced solemnly, "when a man realizes the error of his ways."

Shana nodded again. She wished she'd talked to her friend weeks ago; Catherine saw everything with such clarity and insight.

"Are you tempted to take him back?"

"Not at all…" She let the rest fade.

"You're sure?"

"Yes, but…" The thought had only occurred to her now. "Until I talk to him…" Even as she said the words, Shana knew that a telephone conversation wouldn't be enough. She needed to see Brad, talk to him in person, which she hadn't really done, not after that one dramatic scene when she'd confronted him with what she knew about Sylvia. Then she'd gone to Seattle to think. She'd phoned him, but hadn't spoken to him in person. Shana had never honestly explained her dissatisfaction with the relationship—aside from the Sylvia issue—nor had she made clear that reconciliation was out of the question. Her severing of the relationship wasn't a ploy to get him back. And it wasn't something she'd done on a whim.

Shana looked at Catherine.

"Actually," Catherine said, "I think talking to Brad is a good idea."

"I do, too." Shana removed her apron and carelessly tossed it over the back of a chair. "Can you take over for me?"

"Now?" Catherine asked, seemingly surprised at how quickly Shana was acting.

"Please. I'll take Jazmine to Portland with me."

"I'll need to call Louis, but I'm pretty sure he hasn't got anything planned for the next few days. Let me find out." She walked over to the phone, and after just a minute's discussion, replaced the receiver. "He said he'd be delighted."

"Good." Her decision made, her resolve strong, Shana went outside to collect Jazmine.

"One question," Catherine said, stopping her on her way out the door. "What do you want me to say if Adam phones?"

That wasn't likely to happen, but she certainly didn't want her friend to divulge that she'd gone off to see Brad. "Our last conversation ended kind of badly, so I doubt—"

"You said that earlier," Catherine broke in, "but I bet he'll be phoning soon. He probably regrets how things went as much as you do."

Shana did regret it and although she hadn't said so, Catherine had intuitively known. "Tell him I'm visiting an old friend out of town." It would be the truth, because she planned to call Gwen Jackson as soon as she got home. As she spoke, Shana absently watched a delivery truck pull into the parking space in front of the restaurant.

The bell above the door jangled cheerfully, and

Catherine hurried out of the kitchen. Shana followed her, sorry their conversation had been interrupted.

All she saw was a large FedEx box.

"Shana Berrie?" the delivery man asked.

Catherine gestured toward Shana.

"I'm Shana," she responded, trying to remember if she'd recently ordered anything that would come by overnight courier. She couldn't think of a thing.

Jazmine trailed the delivery man inside. "What's that?" she asked excitedly.

"I don't know yet." Shana signed the clipboard and yanked the tab at the end of the box. The sender's name was that of a floral company in... It started with a *W* but a large smudge obscured the rest of the word.

"It's probably from Brad," Jazmine muttered disdainfully. "I told you he wants you back."

"No way," Shana said, shaking her head. Anything he had to send her wouldn't come in a box. She'd been waiting for a small jewelry box from him long enough to guarantee that.

When the carton was open, two orchid leis slid onto the counter. Waikiki—that was it. Hawaii. Well, that was one puzzle solved. Catherine gave an immediate gasp of wonder at their delicate beauty.

"Uncle Adam," Jazmine burst out in a squeal of unrestrained delight.

"Is there a card?" Catherine asked.

Shana searched the inside of the box and found it. *"To my two favorite girls. I miss you. Adam."*

Jazmine draped one of the leis over her shoulders, beaming with joy.

Shana wasn't nearly as pleased. "That was a cowardly thing to do," she declared. Just leave it to a man to let flowers do his talking for him. Well, she'd deal with Adam later, but at the moment she had another man on her mind, and that was Brad Moore.

Chapter Nineteen

Shana felt as if she was on a mission now. What Catherine had said was so true—it was as difficult to let go of the expectations created by a relationship as the relationship itself. She needed to complete the process of disconnecting herself from Brad.

The minute she arrived home, Shana instructed Jazmine to pack an overnight bag.

"Where are we going?" Jazmine asked, catching Shana's enthusiasm. The lei still hung around her neck. Shana wore hers, too. She appreciated Adam's gesture, but not as much as she would have if he'd e-mailed or phoned her first. She didn't *want* to think about him now, and yet it was impossible not to. The orchids wafted a lovely scent, reminding her of Adam and their shared kisses.

"To Portland."

"Portland?" Jazmine moaned. "Why are we going *there?*"

Shana already had her suitcase out of her closet and open on top of her bed. She didn't need much—her pajamas, a set of clothes and clean underwear. Her toiletries and makeup. That was it.

"Aunt Shana…"

She whirled around, almost forgetting Jazmine was in the room. "I'm sorry. You asked me why we're going to Portland." The girl deserved the truth. "I need to talk to Brad."

"Brad!" Her niece spit out the name as if she had a bug in her mouth. "Why?" she cried with such a shocked look that Shana nearly laughed. "You're wearing Uncle Adam's lei and you want to visit *Brad?*"

"I need to talk to him."

"But why?"

"It's important," was all Shana could tell her.

"You're not going back to him, are you?" Jazmine's eyes pleaded with hers.

"No. Now pack an overnight bag. I want to head out as soon as we can." Shana had no intention of being away from the business for more than twenty-four hours. She'd already called Gwen and left a message, asking if she could put them up for the night. If not, they'd get a hotel room—a reasonably priced one. The trip would be an adventure, and Shana would make an effort to see that Jazmine had fun. If there was time, they'd stop at Jensen Beach to shop and play tourist. Her niece would enjoy that.

Jazmine hesitated in the doorway. "You're sure about this?"

"Very sure." This was a conversation she should've had with Brad when she left him.

"Are you still in love with Brad?" Jazmine asked urgently, staring up at her.

"No. I told you that."

Jazmine frowned, apparently not entirely convinced. "Do you always do stuff like this?"

"You mean act on impulse?" Shana clarified. She didn't think she did, but she realized she was only beginning to know herself. Buying the ice-cream parlor had been the first impulsive thing she'd done in years. Now this. Perhaps it came from a new sense of having control over her own life.

"Are you packed?" Shana asked, knowing very well that she wasn't.

"Not yet." Her niece dawdled for another few minutes. "I don't think I can leave," she said with a shrug. "My garden needs watering, and Uncle Adam said it's important to give the plants a drink every morning and every night." A smile raised the edges of her mouth. "He said I should sing to them, but nothing too fast or with a strong beat."

Shana smiled, too. "I think they can go without water for a day. You can make it up to them later and give them an extra drink and sing a few lullabies."

Jazmine still hesitated, then finally appeared to reach a decision. She went into her own bedroom.

It seemed to take her niece forever to assemble what she needed. When she reappeared, she was dragging her backpack behind her as if it weighed fifty pounds. "We can go now," she said with an undisguised lack of enthusiasm.

"Good." Shana stood by the car, waiting impatiently. She wondered if Jazmine had transferred the entire contents of her dresser into her backpack, but decided against asking.

"Everything locked up?" Shana had checked the back door and the windows.

Jazmine nodded, climbed into the car while Shana heaved her backpack into the trunk, and fastened her seat belt. Then she sighed heavily.

Shana walked around to the driver's side. "Think of this as an adventure," she said in a breezy voice.

Jazmine's chin drooped to her chest. "Are you going to tell Uncle Adam what you did?"

Involuntarily Shana fingered the lei. "I don't know. Maybe."

"What if Brad gets you to move back to Portland?"

"That won't happen," Shana promised, hiding a smile.

"I just don't understand why it's so important for you to see him again," Jazmine whined. "You said it was over. You said you didn't want to have anything to do with him again. You said—"

"I know what I said." Shana cut her off, started the car and pulled away from the curb.

Jazmine was quiet for the first few minutes. "Where will we stay the night?" she asked.

"At a friend's place."

"What friend?"

"Gwen. You haven't met her."

"Does she have kids?"

"No," Shana murmured as she merged onto the West Seattle freeway and toward Interstate 5.

"Do I get to come along when you talk to Brad?"

Shana hadn't actually considered that, but the answer wasn't difficult. "Probably not."

Jazmine's shoulders slumped forward. "That's what I figured."

"Jazz, this *isn't* what you think. I'm going to see Brad to tell him something…." Only now were her thoughts catching up with her actions.

"What?" Jazmine asked, looking at her for the first time since she got into the car.

"To tell him I made the right decision when I left Portland."

"You mean you're not *sure?*" Her niece seemed about to burst into tears.

"No. Why are you so worried?"

Jazmine stared out the passenger window as if the concrete freeway interchanges were the most fascinating scenery in the world. "Brad phoned, and I told you and then…then you and Uncle Adam had an argument, and now you're driving to Portland. I'm not stupid, you know. I can connect the dots."

"Well, you're looking at the wrong picture." Shana could understand why Jazmine had reached those conclusions but they weren't correct. "You don't need to be concerned, Jazz. I promise."

"I want you to marry Uncle Adam. Don't you want to?"

"Let me deal with one man at a time, okay?" At the moment Adam was the last person she wanted to think about. "Once I talk to Brad, you and I can discuss your uncle Adam."

"Oh, sure," Jazmine muttered. "You don't have to explain anything to *me*. I'm just a kid," she said sarcastically.

Shana sighed. Jazmine really ought to enroll in a drama class because she clearly had talent. In fact, maybe they could find one when they got back….

"Did you mention this to Mom?" Jazmine asked after a precious few moments of silence.

Shana kept her eyes on the road. "There wasn't time to e-mail her."

"Does your friend have a computer I can use?"

"I'm sure she does."

"I'll let Mom know where we are and what you're doing." Jazmine announced this with a great deal of satisfaction.

"Fine." Shana just bet the nine-year-old would delight in letting her mother know they were in Portland. Smiling, she wondered how Jazmine would embellish the tale.

"What if he isn't there?"

Uh-oh. "You mean Brad?" Not once had Shana stopped to consider that. "I…I don't know." This wasn't a situation in which she'd be comfortable leaving behind her newly printed business card. If Brad learned she'd come by his office, or even his condo, he'd assume the wrong thing.

"He has to be there," she said aloud. "He just has to."

Adam checked his watch and calculated the time in Seattle. Three-thirty. The leis should have arrived by now, according to the delivery schedule. He imagined Shana's surprise and pleasure at opening the box and discovering the leis. The orchids were supposed to pave the way for part two of his reconciliation plan—a phone call.

He wasn't sure how it had happened, but somehow his previous conversation with Shana had gone in completely the wrong direction. He certainly hadn't intended to become embroiled in an argument. He couldn't even figure out what kind of mistake he'd made. Whatever it was, he sincerely hoped she was over it by now.

Adam had talked to one of his friends about Shana's reaction. John, another lieutenant commander, had said his wife always started an argument before he left. Apparently it was common among Navy wives. For whatever reason, women found it easier to send their men off to sea if they were upset with them about something. Adam didn't understand it, but John claimed their disagreement was simply Shana's way of letting him know she was in love with him.

That had taken Adam by surprise. *Shana loved him?* Shana loved him! He chose to believe it because he so badly wanted to. He wasn't much of a romantic, but the thought of Shana waiting for him back in Seattle made him happy in a way he'd never experienced before.

He hurried home to make the call in privacy. When he didn't think he could bear to wait another minute, he reached for the telephone and punched out the number for the ice-cream parlor. Leaning back on his sofa, feet stretched out on the coffee table, he listened to the ringing of the phone.

"Olsen's Ice Cream and Pizza Parlor."

The man's voice shook Adam. "Who's this?"

"Who's this?" the male voice echoed.

Adam dropped his stocking feet to the floor and leaned forward far enough to prop his elbows on his knees. "Is Shana there?"

"No. Who's calling, please?"

"Lieutenant Commander Adam Kennedy."

"Oh, hello." The voice instantly became friendly. "This is Louis, Catherine's husband. I'd better let you talk to her. Hold on."

"Should I call back later?"

"No, no, it's fine. Here's Cath."

A couple of seconds later, Shana's number-one employee was on the line. "Adam, hello." She sounded slightly breathless. "What can I do for you?"

"I actually called to talk to Shana."

She paused a telltale moment. "I'm sorry, but you missed her. Shana took Jazmine on a…short vacation."

Adam's disappointment was keen. "Did the leis arrive?" Those had cost him a pretty penny, and he hoped they weren't sitting in a box wilting before Shana even had a chance to see them.

"Oh, yes, and she was…pleased. Jazmine, too."

"Did she mention where she was going?" Perhaps he should try reaching her on her cell. He'd just assumed she'd be at the restaurant.

"Yes, yes, she did," Catherine said. She seemed distracted; either Adam had phoned at a bad time or she was reluctant to tell him exactly where Shana had gone.

"I'll try her cell," he murmured.

"You could do that, of course," Catherine agreed politely. "But…but she might be out of reach."

"Why? Did they drive into the mountains?"

"Uh, no."

Her hesitation made him suspicious. "The ocean?"

"No, ah—listen, I need to go…. There are customers waiting."

"Catherine," Adam said softly. She was hiding something, and he wanted to know what.

"I'll tell Shana you phoned."

"You said Jazmine's with her?"

"Of course she is," Catherine answered sharply.

"What's going on there?" Adam demanded. "Where's Shana?"

Catherine sighed deeply. "I told her. The minute she

said she was leaving, I told Shana you'd phone. Sure enough, here I am, having to tell you."

"Tell me what?"

"Shana's in Portland, visiting a friend. Gwen—a female friend." She spoke with finality, as though she hoped that was the end of his questions.

"Portland?" A chill raced down Adam's arms, one that had nothing to do with the tropical breeze coming through the sliding glass door. "I don't suppose this has anything to do with Brad?"

"You'll have to ask her that." Catherine sighed again. "I refuse to incriminate myself—or her."

Adam snorted. "I see."

Dammit, he did see—and he wasn't enjoying the view.

Chapter Twenty

Shana's stomach tensed with anxiety. What had been a brilliant idea that morning seemed utterly ridiculous now. She waited inside the lobby of Brad's office building, pacing back and forth, trying to put words to the mangled feelings inside her head. She was *not* looking for a reconciliation. But Catherine's insight had made her aware that she'd abandoned her previous life without really settling matters with Brad. There were things that had to be said…except now, all she could think about was Adam.

Thankfully Jazmine was safely ensconced at Gwen's. Her friend was a nurse who worked the night shift; she was up and about when Shana and Jazmine arrived on her front porch. As soon as she heard the reason for Shana's visit, she'd sent her off with a pep talk. Gwen's encouragement had carried Shana all the way to downtown Portland.

However, Shana's resolve had quickly waned when she stepped inside the luxurious lobby. All of a sudden, her tongue felt glued to the roof of her mouth, and when someone casually walked past and greeted her, her returning "good afternoon" came out sounding like "goonoon."

Mortified, Shana hurried into the ladies' room and locked herself inside a stall. She hadn't even bothered to change clothes. Filled with purpose, she'd driven to Portland in shorts and a T-shirt with a smudge of chocolate ice cream on the hem. She was about to have one of the most important conversations of her life, and she resembled someone trying out for clown school.

Sitting on the toilet seat, Shana buried her face in her hands. What was she thinking? She was astonished at her own audacity and horrified at this latest example of impulsive behavior.

Her goal, when she left Seattle in a heated frenzy, had been to make Brad Moore realize what he'd lost—and whose fault that was. She was going to end the relationship properly, definitively, for her own sake, and ultimately for his, too. After coming this far, she refused to turn back. She'd simply buy something appropriate. There was time.

That decision made, Shana walked into an ultra-expensive boutique in the lobby. Either the sales clerk took pity on her or she was afraid Shana was about to shoplift a mannequin, because she immediately shot out from behind the cash register.

"Can I help you?"

"Can you ever." Shana threw herself on the mercy of a complete stranger. "I need an outfit that'll make a man rue the day he—"

"Say no more." The clerk raised her hand. "I have just the dress." She looked Shana up and down. "Size four?"

Maybe ten years ago. "Six," she muttered.

"Four. This dress is expensive enough to be a four."

Shana laughed. She didn't care how much it cost; her ego was at stake.

Once she stood in front of the mirror, Shana barely recognized the woman staring back at her. The knee-length floral dress was simple yet elegant, fanning out at her waist in pleats that emphasized her hips and long legs.

"Wow," she whispered, impressed. She didn't even glance at the price tag. It was better not to know.

The clerk nodded approvingly. "Perfect."

Shana twisted around to take a gander at the back and decided that view was even sexier. She hoped Brad took a good, long look when she walked away.

Not wanting to show up clutching a bag with her shorts and T-shirt inside—that kind of contradicted the classy image—she ditched her old clothes.

The only unfortunate part of the new outfit was the matching shoes. The one pair left was a full size too small for Shana, but the slinky sandals were gorgeous. With a minimum of regret, she purchased them anyway. By the time she walked out of the boutique, her little toe on each shoe had squeezed between the narrow straps and escaped. She'd be fine as long as Brad didn't look at her feet.

Shana was still testing her ability to walk when the elevator opened and Brad Moore entered the lobby. Swallowing her breath, Shana nearly choked when Brad saw her. He stopped abruptly, his shock unmistakable.

"Shana," he cried. He held out his arms to her, surprise replaced by delight. "You look fabulous."

"Yes, I do." Now wasn't the time for modesty, especially in light of what she'd paid for this outfit.

She tilted her head to one side and allowed him to kiss her cheek.

"What are you doing here?"

No need to beat around the bush. "I came to see you."

"Great." He didn't bother to hide his enthusiasm. "Shall we have a drink somewhere and talk?"

"That would be fine." She played it cool, refusing to let him see how flustered she was.

Taking her by the elbow, Brad led the way out of the high-rise office tower. Shana struggled to keep up with him, the too-tight shoes pinching her feet unmercifully. Her little toes hung over the edge of the shoes and she prayed no one would notice. Thankfully there was a hotel bar across the street.

Brad led her to a small table, ordered them each a glass of merlot and grinned at her as if she were a delectable dessert.

The cocktail waitress brought their wine and Brad sent a flirtatious glance in her direction.

Once he'd finished paying for their drinks, he smiled at her confidently. "You got my message?"

"You mean the one you weren't willing to say to me yourself?"

He had the good grace to look embarrassed. "I would have if you'd been home. Who is that kid, anyway?"

Shana was surprised Jazmine hadn't enlightened him. "My niece. You remember my sister, Alison, don't you? Jazmine is her daughter."

"I met your sister once, right?" Brad raised both eyebrows. "The kid's got attitude."

He hadn't seen anything yet.

"How've you been?" he asked, but before she could respond he added, "I've missed you."

This was where—according to his script—she was supposed to tell him how lonely she'd been without him and how much she regretted the things she'd said and done.

He waited, and when she didn't immediately offer the desired response, he frowned. "I'm glad you're here. We have a lot to discuss."

"I came because—"

Brad reached for her hand, stopping her. "You don't need to say it. We both made mistakes and we're both sorry. Let's leave it at that."

"You think I made a mistake?"

"That's why you're here, isn't it?"

She took her first sip of wine and let its smoothness flow over her tongue. "I came because when I walked out on you, I was angry and hurt."

"I know…"

"I don't feel either of those things anymore. I wanted to look you in the eye, see what I used to find so attractive." She sighed. Whatever it was had long vanished. "I really just came, Brad, to clear the air once and for all, and to do it properly."

Brad's expression changed and he stared at her. "You are coming back to Portland, aren't you?"

She loved this city and missed her job. The ice-cream parlor demanded constant attention and supervision. The hours were long and the financial compensation small. As a pharmaceutical salesperson, she'd been able to leave work at the end of the day and not give her job another thought. Having a business of her own was a completely different proposition. The ice-cream and pizza parlor had seemed like an escape from an unhappy situation, but for the first time, she wondered if she'd made the right decision.

"Shana?" Brad asked, breaking into her musings.

"Portland? I don't know," she admitted honestly.

"You love me, don't you?" He asked the question but she could tell he wasn't as sure of himself as he'd been earlier.

Seeing the crack in his confidence weakened her resolve. "That's just it," Shana said. "I loved you so completely and I was so sure you loved me."

"I do love you," Brad insisted. "I know you were upset and you had every right to be. I was a fool, but I swear to you it'll never happen again. I regretted it immediately. I was sick that I lost you because of Sylvia."

Shana didn't trust him enough to believe his promises.

He seemed to be debating how much of the truth to reveal. "We went out two or three times, but that's beside the point. It didn't take me long to realize I'd made the biggest mistake of my life. It's *you* I love, Shana. It's you I want to be with."

The complete absence of the word *marriage* didn't escape her. In other words, they'd resume their relationship exactly where they'd left off. His script again—but not hers.

Brad must have seen the strength and determination in her eyes. "You mean it, don't you?" he asked morosely. "This really is goodbye."

"Yes."

"But you loved me at one time. I can't believe you don't now."

A sad smile formed but she refused to answer him.

His own smile returned. "You do love me. You wouldn't be here now if you didn't still have feelings for me."

Brad's gaze pleaded with her as he clasped her hand in both of his. "You do love me," he said again.

She remained silent, and all at once he seemed to realize she wasn't changing her mind. That was when he said the one thing that, a few months ago, might have swayed her.

"I want to marry you."

Even that didn't elicit a response.

"I'm sincere, Shana. I couldn't be any more serious. You set the date and the time."

Rather than drag this out, she told him the truth. "I met someone else."

Brad frowned. "Is this the guy your niece mentioned?"

"Yes."

"Certainly didn't take you long, did it?" he asked, sitting back. "So the real reason you're here is to rub my face in it."

"No." Until this moment she hadn't planned to say anything about Adam.

"I thought you were in love with *me*. Pretty fickle, aren't you?"

She smiled, knowing she'd asked for that. "I *was* in love with you, but that's over." She paused. "It's funny, you know."

"I'm not laughing."

She shook her head. "I didn't think it was possible to feel like this about a man on such short acquaintance. Adam's good to me and to my niece.... He's a family friend. That's how we met."

"Bully for you."

"Don't, Brad." She hadn't expected to be this honest with him but it seemed important. She had no intention of being vindictive or mean-spirited. She might not love him anymore, but she didn't begrudge him happiness.

"And what does Adam do?" Brad asked, his words

hard and clipped. "Oh, yes, I remember now. He's some big deal in the Navy." He lifted his brows dismissively. "So. Can you tell me exactly why you're here?"

Shana sipped her wine. "I came here this morning, convinced I had to see you. I already told you why. I felt—and still feel—that I had to end this relationship properly."

Brad closed his eyes for a moment. "Okay. Consider it ended."

"Thank you," she said graciously. "I even went so far as to buy this dress at a price so outrageous I'll be making payments for the next six months." She glanced down at her feet and tried to remember what size shoe her sister wore and hoped it was a seven.

"So this outfit was for my benefit?"

Shana nodded. "I wanted you to be sorry you lost me."

His eyes grew gentle. "I was sorry before you got here. I've been sorry for months."

Despite her mood, she smiled. "That's probably the sweetest thing you've ever said to me."

"So you didn't come here to make me feel bad about you and Popeye?"

Shana inhaled softly. She knew exactly why she'd found it necessary to drive to Portland. "No, I didn't," she said softly. "I came to say goodbye."

Chapter Twenty-One

Adam Kennedy wasn't having a good day. In fact, the entire week was down the septic tank, and he blamed Shana Berrie for that. If she was trying to make him jealous, it was damned well working.

"That's what women do to you," his friend John told him. They sat across from each other at Navy Headquarters for the Pacific Fleet. "They mess with your mind and they make irrational demands. Take my wife, for example. Angie got upset with me because there was a cockroach in the house, as if it's my duty as her husband to rid the place of bugs. Can you believe it? She's afraid of a stupid bug, and if I don't deal with it, I might as well not go home tonight."

Barely hearing his friend's rant, Adam scowled. Shana certainly hadn't wasted any time giving up on him. As far as she was concerned, it seemed to be out of sight, out of mind. Well, fine, great, whatever. If she wanted to race back to lover boy, then that was perfectly fine by him.

The hell it was, Adam decided quickly. He hadn't slept well; his appetite was gone and he had a sick feeling that refused to go away. He didn't know how everything had fallen apart so quickly. In his view they'd *had* a promising relationship, with emphasis on the past tense.

The phone rang and Adam left it for John. What he needed was a bout of hard exercise, but with his shoulder golf was still out of the question and swimming would be just as painful. He could always jog, he supposed, but it wasn't something he enjoyed.

John answered the phone, and Adam watched as his gaze shot across the room. He put the caller on hold. "It's for you. A woman. Says her name is Shana." He gave Adam a significant look, both eyebrows raised.

It took Adam a moment to assimilate that. His pulse accelerated and then immediately slowed. The call was most likely a courtesy to let him know she was going back to lover boy in Portland.

With that in mind, Adam reached for the telephone receiver. He responded in a crisp military tone, keeping his voice devoid of emotion.

"Adam, hello," Shana said, her own voice friendly.

Adam nearly weakened, but he realized she was probably warming him up before she dropped the news. She'd led him on, he mused darkly, and now she was going to make a fool of him.

"I wanted to thank you for the leis. Jazmine and I were thrilled. It was so generous of you."

Adam kept silent, bracing himself.

After an awkward moment, during which he said nothing, Shana said, "I feel badly about the way our last conversation went."

"Forget it," Adam said in the same emotionless tone. He wanted her to think it hardly mattered to him. He should've taken the hint then. Shana was trouble and he'd best get out of this unpredictable relationship. But even as the thought went through his mind, he didn't believe it.

"I blame myself," Shana added, "for picking a fight with you. I was just reacting to your leaving, I guess." She hesitated. "We had so little time, and I knew I was going to miss you so much. Jazmine, too, of course."

John had explained that this was the same reaction he got from his wife, but Adam couldn't really accept that. Why would Shana care whether he was stationed in Hawaii if she was going back to the guy in Portland?

She seemed to realize he wasn't responding. "Are you upset about something?" she asked tentatively.

"Should I be?" He answered her question with one of his own.

"I don't think so." Her voice gained conviction, but gone was the sweet joy he'd heard in her earlier. Now she sounded wary.

"I understand you were out of town," he said, broaching the subject that was foremost on his mind.

His announcement was followed by stark silence. "You know about that?"

"I do. So if you're planning to tell me what I think you are, I'd appreciate if you'd just say it and be done with it."

"Say *what*?"

"You want out," he said flippantly. "So let's just call it quits."

"You're willing to end this without another word?" She seemed shocked—and annoyed.

"I'm not the one who drove down to visit an old lover. You never did say how things went between you and Bernie."

"It's Brad," she corrected. "And you're right, I didn't."

He waited, unwilling to cut off the conversation and at the same time reluctant to continue trading barbs.

"Isn't this all a little silly?" Shana asked.

"When did you decide to go?"

"In the morning. It was a spur-of-the-moment idea. Jazmine and I spent the night with an old friend—an old female friend," she added. "I saw Brad and we talked."

"About what?" He didn't mean to ask and wanted to withdraw the question the moment it left his mouth.

She paused, taking a moment before she answered. "I don't remember if I told you I moved to Seattle in kind of a rush."

"You might've said something like that." He tried to play it cool, but the truth was, he hung on every word.

"So I needed to see Brad."

"I'm sure you did," he muttered, unable to disguise his sarcasm.

His comment generated a lengthy silence. "We had a chance to talk and to say certain things that needed to be said," she finally told him.

She didn't enlighten him as to what those things might be. "So you're back in Seattle?"

"Yes. I have to go now. The only reason I phoned," she said, "is to thank you for the leis. Jazmine and I love them. Now I should get back to work."

Adam had to bite his tongue to keep from pleading

with her to stay on the phone a bit longer. He wished they could start the entire conversation over.

"How's Jazmine?" he asked, using the question as a delaying tactic.

"Fabulous...wonderful. Thank you again for the orchids."

And with that, the line was disconnected. He waited a few seconds while the buzz sounded in his ear. Adam replaced the receiver and glared at the phone as he replayed the conversation. He knew he'd made a number of tactical errors, and that was because his ego had gotten in the way.

"So, how'd it go?" John asked conversationally.

"Not good."

"Sorry to hear that. I told you—women mess with your mind. You should've figured that out by now."

John was right; he should have.

The tension in Adam's stomach didn't diminish all day. At the end of his watch, he returned to his quarters to find the message light on his phone blinking. It was too much to hope that Shana had called him a second time. Holding his breath, he pressed the message button.

Jazmine's voice greeted him. "Uncle Adam, what's with you? You've really blown it now. Call me at the house when you get home. I'll make sure I answer."

Adam reached for the phone. Here he was, conspiring with a nine-year-old. *That* was a sign of desperation.

Chapter Twenty-Two

Ali was quite entertained by the tone of Shana's e-mails in the last week. Her sister was not in a good mood. She'd only brought up Adam's name once, but Ali was well aware that the lieutenant commander was the sole source of Shana's irritation.

Thankfully, Jazmine had been able to fill Ali in. Apparently Adam and Shana had some form of falling-out. Shana had driven to Portland to say a final goodbye to Brad, and Adam was out of sorts about it. From what Jazmine said, they were currently ignoring each other.

Ali didn't usually meddle in other people's romances. She hadn't said anything when Shana was involved with Brad, and she wouldn't interfere now. At least she didn't *think* she would. But those two were perfect together, and it would be a shame if this relationship died because they were too stubborn to admit they were attracted to each other. Although Ali suspected that their feelings had gone way beyond attraction…

Preoccupied, she walked toward the wardroom. She generally ate with the other officers at six every evening, but tonight she was later than usual. Life at sea had grown monotonous, and the days seemed to run into each other without any real break to distinguish one from the next. When she entered the room, there were a few officers at various tables, but she noticed only one.

Commander Frank Dillon.

Ali hadn't seen or talked to him since they'd met in the Farmer's Market in Guam. Just seeing him again gave her pause. She'd thought about their brief conversation that very afternoon; even now she wasn't sure what to make of it. Her friends, too, were full of questions she hadn't been able to answer. Ali filled her tray and started for a table.

"Good evening, Commander," she said, greeting him.

"Ali." He didn't look any too pleased to see her, if his scowl was any indication.

She sat down several tables away, but facing him. It would be utterly rude to present him with her back. "I do hope you've sufficiently recovered." Ali knew she sounded stilted but couldn't help it. She avoided eye contact by reaching for the salt shaker.

"I have, thank you. And you?"

His question caught her unawares. "I haven't been ill, Commander."

"Yes, of course." He stood as if he couldn't leave fast enough and disappeared with such speed, it made her head swim. Clearly she was the last person he wanted to see. Only this time, Ali didn't take offense.

She'd come to the conclusion that she flustered

Commander Dillon, which was a heady sensation. She recalled how gruff and rude he'd been in sick bay and, thanks to their brief conversation on Guam, she finally understood the reason. He'd thought she was married.

The next evening, Alison purposely delayed her meal and arrived at the same time as the night before. Sure enough Frank was there, sitting at the same table, lingering over coffee. He looked up and smiled uncertainly when he saw her.

"Good evening, Commander." She greeted him the same way she had the previous night. After getting her meal, she chose a seat one table closer.

"Lieutenant Commander." His eyes held hers, and he didn't immediately leap up and run away.

"I have a question for you," she said and again reached for the salt shaker. It was a convenient excuse to avert her gaze. She feared he might read her intense interest in him, which seemed to compound after each meeting.

He straightened. "Fire away."

"Do I frighten you?"

He raised one eyebrow. "Truthfully? You terrify me."

"Any particular reason?"

He expelled his breath. "As a matter of fact, there are several. Most of them would get me court-martialed if I mentioned them."

"I see." She didn't really, but she was definitely curious.

"Does that amuse you?" he asked, his face deadpan.

"Commander, are you flirting with me?"

This question seemed to take him aback, and he frowned. "I can assure you I wouldn't know how. Is that what you think I'm doing?"

She shook her head. "I'm not sure, but I do have another question for you."

"All right. I just hope it isn't as difficult as the first." A hint of a smile touched his eyes.

Alison dipped her fork into the creamy mashed potatoes. "I wonder, do you know anything about a bolt of red silk that was delivered to the ship in my name?"

"Red silk?" He shrugged. "I'm afraid I can't help you there."

"That isn't an answer to my question, Commander."

He glanced at his watch, and as if he'd suddenly realized he was late for an important meeting, abruptly stood. He grabbed his coffee cup and took one last swallow before he excused himself and hurried away.

Alison hadn't known what to think when the silk had appeared in her quarters. She was able to track down the petty officer who delivered it, and learned that the man from the market had brought it to the docks. He'd left instructions that it should be taken directly to her. Alison had badly wanted that silk, but the price was more than she'd been willing to pay.

Just before she drifted off to sleep the night before, she'd remembered haggling with the silk merchant just before she'd run into Frank. He must have purchased it for her. It was the only thing that made sense—and yet it didn't. But judging by the way he'd reacted to her questions this evening, she had to wonder.

The following night when Alison arrived at the wardroom, Frank wasn't there. Her heart sank with disappointment. She really didn't have much of an appetite and ate very little of her meal. She'd almost decided against coffee but it was her habit to end her dinner with a cup.

Just when she was ready to leave, uninterested in the

remains of her cooling coffee, Frank rushed in, looking harried.

"Good evening, Commander," Alison said, smiling her welcome. Hiding her pleasure at seeing him had become impossible.

He poured himself a cup of coffee and joined her. This was progress. They'd begun by sitting several tables apart and had drawn closer with each encounter.

He was silent for a few minutes, concentrating on his coffee, methodically adding sugar and cream, then stirring. "You have children?" he asked unexpectedly.

"A nine-year-old daughter."

He nodded.

"Jazmine is living with my sister in Seattle right now."

He nodded again. "Is this the first time you've been apart for so much time?"

"Yes." Then, feeling it was only fair that she be completely honest, Alison said, "This will be my last duty assignment."

"You're leaving the Navy?" He made it sound like an incomprehensible decision.

"My husband loved the Navy the way you do. He couldn't imagine civilian life."

"Can you?" he asked.

"No. But it's something I have to do." The Navy had shaped her life, but now she had to put Jazmine's welfare first. She was proud of how well her daughter had adjusted to a new environment, but a child needed roots and stability. Alison felt obliged to provide that, especially since she'd become, however unwillingly, a single parent.

"Where will you settle?" Frank asked.

"I haven't decided yet. I'm considering Seattle. Jazmine seems to like it there, and it's where my sister lives."

"Is she married?"

"Single," Ali explained. "But she's romantically involved with someone."

Frank stared down into his coffee, cupped between his outstretched hands. "I don't know much about romance." He took a swig of coffee. "I'm pretty much a failure in that department."

"You're divorced, aren't you?" She recalled that he'd told her this.

"A long time now."

Alison studied him as he sipped his coffee. "Given up, have you?"

He raised his head, his gaze burning into hers. "Until recently I had." His shoulders rose as if he was taking in a deep breath. "It's not appropriate to ask now, but I was wondering…I was thinking that in a few months, when you've…resigned your commission, you might consider going to dinner with me. It wouldn't mean anything. I mean, there'd be no obligation on either part, and if you're not ready—"

"Commander," Alison said, breaking into his soliloquy. This was the most he'd ever said to her at one time. "Yes."

"Yes?" He eyed her quizzically.

"I'd be honored to have dinner with you."

He seemed tentative, unbelieving, and Ali smiled.

"More than honored," she added softly and reached for her own coffee. She needed a sip to ease the dryness in her mouth and throat.

"It won't be for several months," he warned.

"I'm well aware of that, Commander."

He sighed and looked away. "Don't take this personally, but it's not a good idea for us to continue meeting here."

Disappointment hit her hard. "Why not?" Their meetings were completely innocent. This was the third night in a row, and not once had they even touched.

"Lieutenant Commander," Frank said, his voice barely above a whisper. "You tempt me and while I'm a disciplined man, I don't think I can hold back my feelings for you indefinitely. Give me a date and a time I can meet you in Seattle and I'll be there."

Alison met his eyes and smiled. "January twenty-seventh. One o'clock in the afternoon. At the bronze pig in Pike Place Market."

She'd chosen the date a bit recklessly, perhaps, but that was Peter's birthday, which made it easy to remember. And she was very sure Peter would approve….

Chapter Twenty-Three

"Aren't you going to call Uncle Adam?" Jazmine was pestering Shana for about the hundredth time that week.

"Why should I?" Shana muttered, scooping ice cream from the bottom of the caramel pecan container and packing what remained into a quart-size one. This was her life these days. For at least two hours every day, she risked frostbite with her face in the freezer.

"You know," she said, righting herself and holding up the ice-cream scoop for emphasis, "when I moved to Seattle, I decided I was finished with men. I didn't need a man in my life then and I don't need one now. I'm better off without them."

Jazmine sat on the other side of the counter, her chin propped in her hands. Shana noticed that she was frowning.

"We don't need boys?"

"We don't," Shana reiterated.

"At all?"

"Well, technically we do, but only for reproductive purposes." This was definitely an area she didn't want to get into with a nine-year-old.

"But aren't they kind of fun to have around?"

She realized she was tainting her niece's mind because of her own negative experiences. That had to stop. Besides, Adam had potential—or he did when he wasn't overtaken by jealousy. The thing was, he had absolutely nothing to be jealous about. It was almost as if he *wanted* to be upset with her. Fine, then, she'd just let him.

"Men have their uses," Shana replied guardedly.

"I thought you liked Uncle Adam."

"I do…I did…I do." While Shana was still annoyed with Adam, she missed him, too. That was the point. She didn't want to think about him, but she couldn't help it—which annoyed her even more.

"You should call him," Jazmine suggested again.

Shana refused to do that. "I phoned last time. It's his turn."

"Oh." Her niece sounded distressed.

"What's wrong?" Shana asked, unsure what had brought the woebegone expression to Jazmine's face.

Jazmine sighed deeply. "I was just hoping you liked Uncle Adam the same way he likes you."

Now Shana was the one frowning. "I do like him. It's just that two people don't always see eye-to-eye." This was difficult enough to explain to an adult, let alone a child. "Sometimes it's best to simply leave things alone."

"It is?" Jazmine squinted as though confused. "Is that how you felt about Brad?"

Shana thought for a moment, then nodded. "Yes, in the beginning. When I first broke up with him."

"But you went to see him again 'cause you didn't like the way it ended, right?"

"Right. I regretted the fact that I'd run off in a fit of righteous indignation. It was over, and I wanted him to know that in a civilized manner."

"You aren't being impulsive now? About not phoning Uncle Adam?"

Coming out from behind the counter, Shana slid onto the stool next to her niece. Sighing expressively, she said, "You're pretty smart for a kid."

Jazmine flashed her a bright smile. "How come?"

"You just are." Her niece had told her what she needed to hear. She'd refused to phone Adam strictly out of pride. Their last conversation had been painful. She'd been lighthearted and hopeful when she called him, but his gruff responses had short-circuited her joy. He hadn't phoned her since and she hadn't phoned him, either. They were behaving like children.

"That's what I don't understand," Jazmine murmured, returning to her original pose, chin cupped in her hands, elbows splayed. "You went to talk to Brad, but you won't go see Uncle Adam."

"He's in Hawaii." It wasn't like he was a three-hour drive down the interstate. "It isn't that easy to get to Hawaii."

"Don't they have ninety-nine-dollar flights there?"

"I doubt it." More than likely it would be five hundred dollars. Shana sat up. Then again, going to see him in Hawaii might help clear up this misunderstanding—

resolve this stalemate—and she wanted that. She believed he did, too. One of them had to make the first move and it might as well be her.

Shana was shocked at herself. She was actually considering this. She'd spent all that money on the dress she'd worn to see Brad, and now she was about to spend more. She supposed she could always wear her new dress when—if—she went to see Adam. Why not?

"You could check the computer," Jazmine said confidently. "There are advertisements on TV all the time about airfare deals over the Internet."

"You think I should?"

Jazmine nodded eagerly. "If you find a cheap ticket to Hawaii, you should go."

"I can't close the restaurant."

"You don't need to close it. Catherine ran it when we went to Portland," Jazmine reminded her. "And that was just to see Brad."

She opened her mouth to claim that seeing Brad was different. Well…it was and it wasn't. She'd been willing to make arrangements and a few sacrifices in order to talk to him. And she cared about Adam a hundred times more than she did Brad.

"Remember Tim, the single dad who wanted to go out with you?" Jazmine asked.

"Yes. Why?"

"I saw him in the park. He's back with his wife and he said it was because of you."

"Me?"

"Yup—he said you were the one who told him he was still in love with her. He knew you were right but the hardest part was telling Heather—that's her name. He's really glad he did, though."

"I'm glad, too. But why are you—"

Before Shana could finish the question, Jazmine blurted out her reply. "Because the hardest part is you telling Uncle Adam how you feel—so do it!"

"I will." Shana closed her eyes. She wanted this relationship with Adam to work. All the years she'd been with Brad, friends and co-workers had said he didn't deserve her, and she'd refused to listen. Now the people she loved and respected most were telling her that Adam was a dream come true—and once again she hadn't been listening. But that was about to change.

"It all depends on whether Louis and Catherine can work while we're away," Shana murmured, biting her bottom lip.

"They can," Jazmine said immediately. "They love it here. And if you marry Uncle Adam, they want to buy the business." She leaned close and whispered conspiratorially, "I heard them talking about it."

Now that the idea had taken root, Shana was convinced it was the right thing to do. She knew that if she sat down with Adam for five minutes, they'd get past the false impressions and false pride. She wanted him in her life; it was that simple.

"We're going to Hawaii?" Jazmine asked, her look expectant.

Shana smiled and slowly nodded. Yes, they were going to Hawaii. Adam might think this relationship was over, but she wasn't willing to lose out on her best chance for happiness yet. If everything went as she prayed it would, she just might end up with a Navy husband.

Adam's bad mood hadn't improved in a week. A dozen times, probably more, he'd lifted the receiver to call

Shana. This estrangement was his fault. But for reasons he didn't want to examine, he'd been reluctant to phone.

Okay, it was time to own up to the truth. He'd been waiting for her to break down and phone *him*. After more than a week, he might as well accept that it wasn't going to happen.

"You feeling better?" John asked when Adam arrived at the office Friday morning.

"I don't know." He shook his head. "What do you think are my chances of hitching a transport to Seattle this weekend?"

John perked up. "You're going to see her?"

Adam nodded. As best as he could figure, this was the only way he and Shana would ever make any progress. He was ready to take responsibility for his part in this fiasco and admit he'd overreacted. After all, she'd said it was over between her and this Bernie character.

From today, from this moment forward, he chose to believe her. His next task was to tell her he'd been wrong. He didn't like apologizing, but having Shana in his life was worth a few minutes of humiliation.

"This *is* good news," John said, grinning broadly. "Finally."

Adam leaned back in his chair. He'd get to Seattle one way or another, even if it meant paying for a commercial flight.

"Are you going to let her know you're coming?" John asked.

"No."

"So you're going to surprise her?"

"I believe I will," he said, already deep in thought.

He pictured the reunion: Shana would be at the ice-cream parlor with a dozen kids all placing their orders at once. She was great with kids, great with Jazmine, patient and generous.

She'd be scooping ice cream for all those kids, and then she'd look up and there he'd be, standing in the doorway. He'd wear his uniform. Women were said to like a man in uniform, and Adam decided he needed all the help he could get.

He returned to his imagined scenario. Naturally Shana would be astonished to see him; she might even drop the ice-cream scoop. Their eyes would meet, and everything else in the room would fade as she came around the counter and walked into his embrace. Adam's arms suddenly ached with the need to hold her. Until this very minute, he hadn't realized just how badly he wanted Shana in his life. He'd felt the need to link his life with a woman's earlier that summer, and that need had grown stronger, more irresistible, ever since he'd met Shana.

"You really think surprising her is such a great idea?" John asked skeptically.

"Of course it is," Adam said. Why wouldn't it be?

Chapter Twenty-Four

"I am so bummed," Jazmine muttered, sitting in front of the computer after e-mailing her mother.

Shana was disappointed, too, but she tried not to let it show. She'd spent half her day on the Internet, searching for last-minute bargain tickets to Honolulu. Apparently there was no such thing. It didn't matter what she could or would have been willing to pay. There simply weren't any seats available for the next few days. The best rates were for the following week.

"Waiting a week won't be so bad," Shana assured her niece.

"We should let Uncle Adam know we're coming."

That meant Shana would have to pick up the phone and call him, which was something she hadn't managed to do in more than two weeks. Jazmine was right, though. It probably wasn't fair just to land on his doorstep and expect everything to fall neatly into place.

The doorbell rang and Jazmine was out of the computer chair and racing to the front door. Shana walked briskly behind her, uncomfortable with the girl flinging open the door without first checking to see who was there.

Her worries were for nothing. Jazmine stood on the tips of her toes, peering through the tiny peephole. She stared for the longest moment, then her shoulders sagged and she backed away. "It's for you," she said in a disappointed voice.

Shana moved in front of her niece and opened the door. She was in no mood to deal with a salesman or a nuisance call. When she found Adam Kennedy standing on the other side, she was stunned into speechlessness.

"Adam?" His name was a mere wisp of sound. He looked good, no, better than good. *Great.* He was a thousand times more compelling than she remembered, and her heart felt in danger of bursting right then and there. If their disagreement had given him a minute's concern, his face didn't reveal it. He seemed rested and relaxed.

He smiled, and Shana's knees started to shake. It shouldn't be like this, the rational part of her mind inserted. She shouldn't be this happy to see him or this excited. But she was.

"Can I come in?"

"Sure." Jazmine was the one who answered. The nine-year-old slipped around Shana and held open the screen door. Judging by the broad smile on the girl's face, anyone might think she was ushering in Santa Claus.

Shana frowned. "You knew about this?" she asked her niece.

Jazmine shook her head, denying any knowledge. "But I fooled you, didn't I? You didn't guess it was Adam." Then she grinned at the man in question. "We were coming to see you, only we couldn't get a flight for this weekend. We have tickets for next week."

"You were flying to Hawaii to see me?" Adam's eyes probed Shana's.

She nodded, and found the shock of seeing him in the room with her nearly overwhelming. Placing her hand on her chest, she felt her heart hammer against her palm. Even with the evidence standing right in front of her, she had a hard time taking it in.

Reaching for Adam's hand, Jazmine led him into the living room. "You can sit if you want."

Adam chose the sofa.

"You, too, Aunt Shana," Jazmine said, orchestrating events as though she were moving figures on a chessboard. She took Shana's hand next and led her to the overstuffed chair.

"Okay," Jazmine said, standing in the middle of the room between them. "You two need to talk. I can go to my room or I can stay and supervise."

Shana's gaze didn't waver from Adam's. "Your room," she murmured, hardly able to catch her breath.

"Your room," Adam echoed.

"Really?" Jazmine's frustration echoed in her voice.

"Go." Shana pointed down the hall, although her eyes were still on Adam. She was afraid that if she glanced away he might disappear.

Jazmine started to walk in the direction of her bedroom. "I'm leaving my door open, and if I hear any yelling, I'm coming right back. Okay?"

Adam's mouth quivered with the beginnings of a smile. "Okay."

After Jazmine left, there was a moment of awkward silence—and then they both started to speak at once.

"I'm so sorry…."

"I'm an idiot…" Adam held up his hand and gestured for her to go first.

Shana moved to the edge of the cushion, clasping her hands together. "Oh, Adam, I'm so *sorry.* I wanted to call you, I really did. I thought about it so many times."

"I was afraid of losing you."

"That won't happen," she told him. "Don't you know how I feel about you?"

When he didn't reply, she said, "I wasn't planning to fall in love again, but—"

"You love me?" he interrupted.

Shana hadn't meant to declare her feelings so soon, and certainly not like this. The way she'd envisioned the scene, it would be a romantic moment over dinner and champagne, not in the middle of her small rental house, with her niece standing in the bedroom doorway listening to every word.

"She does," Jazmine answered for Shana. "She's been impossible ever since you went to Hawaii."

"Jazmine," Shana warned.

"Sorry," the girl muttered.

"Maybe it'd be best if you closed your door," Adam suggested.

Jazmine stamped her foot and shouted "Okay," but when Shana's gaze shot down the hallway, she noticed that her niece's bedroom door was only halfway shut.

"You were saying?" Adam said and motioned for her to continue.

"I forget where I was."

"I believe you'd just declared your undying love for me. I'd like to hear more."

"I'm sure you would," she said, smiling despite their interruptions, "but I was thinking it would be good to hear how you feel, too."

"You will, I promise," Adam assured her, "but I'd appreciate if you finished your thoughts first. You were saying you hadn't planned to fall in love…"

Shana lowered her eyes. It was difficult to think clearly when she was looking at Adam. The effect he had on her was that powerful. "I think sometimes love finds you when you least expect it. As you might've guessed, my opinion of the opposite sex was somewhere in the basement when I came to Seattle. And then Jazmine arrived. At first I envied the easy relationship you two shared. And my sister couldn't stop singing your praises."

"You weren't in the mood to hear anything positive about a man. Any man."

"Exactly," Shana concurred. "But you were so patient with Jazmine and…you were patient with me, too."

"I was attracted to you from the moment we met."

"Really?"

"You knocked my socks off." They both grinned at that. Then his expression grew serious again. "Having this surgery wasn't a pleasant experience." He pressed his hand gently to his shoulder. "I was in pain, and my life felt empty, and all of a sudden you were on the scene. I felt as soon as we met that I could love you."

"You did?" Her voice lifted with joy.

"And I do love you. I recognized that I had to give you time. Coming out of a long-term relationship, you were bound to need an adjustment period. I understood that. But I don't think you have any idea how badly I wanted to be with you."

"You love me," she repeated, hardly hearing anything else he'd said. "You love me!"

"I know you wanted to marry Bernie—"

"It's Brad, and no…not anymore."

"Good, because I'm hoping you'll marry me."

Jazmine's bedroom door flew open. "Aunt Shana, say yes. I beg of you, say yes!"

"Jazmine!" Shana and Adam shouted simultaneously.

"Okay, okay," the nine-year-old moaned and retreated back inside her bedroom.

Adam hesitated only briefly. "Well, what do you think?"

"You mean about us getting married?" Just saying the words produced an inner happiness that radiated from her heart to every single part of her. "Being your wife would make me the happiest woman alive."

Adam stood and she met him halfway. Seconds later, they were locked in each other's arms and his mouth was on hers. From the way he kissed her, she knew he'd been telling the truth. He loved her! After several deep kisses, Adam raised his head and framed her face with both hands. His eyes bored intently into hers.

"One question, and if my asking offends you, I apologize in advance. I need to know something."

"Anything."

His eyes flickered with uncertainty. "Why was it necessary to talk to Ber—Brad?"

Shana sighed and kissed his jaw. "I wanted to say goodbye to him properly."

"And you intended to see me next week."

She nodded, then caught the lobe of his ear between her teeth and gently bit down on the soft flesh. The shiver that went through him encouraged her to further exploration.

"What were you going to say to me?" he asked, his voice a husky whisper.

"Hmm…" she responded, her thoughts clouded with desire. "Hello, and that I'm crazy in love with you."

"Good answer." Adam directed his mouth back to hers, and soon they were deeply involved in another kiss.

The sound of a throat being cleared broke into Shana's consciousness several seconds later.

"Did you two forget something?" Jazmine asked, hands on her hips. "Like *me?*"

Shana buried her face in Adam's shoulder.

"Howdy, squirt," he managed in a voice Shana barely recognized as his.

"This is all very good, but we have a wedding to plan, you know."

"A wedding?" Shana lifted her head and murmured, "We have plenty of time to work on that."

"I don't think so," Jazmine insisted. "We'll be in Hawaii next week. We should do it then. Let's get this show on the road!"

"Next week?" Shana looked questioningly at Adam, not sure that arranging a wedding in such a short time was even possible.

"Would you be willing?" he asked, catching Jazmine's enthusiasm.

Shana nodded. "Of course, but only if Ali can be there. I want her at our wedding."

Adam brought her close. "I do, too."

Jazmine applauded loudly. "I know it isn't good manners to say I told you so," she announced with smug satisfaction, "but this time I can't help it."

"We'll let you," Adam said, his arms around Shana. "Because this time you're absolutely right."

Shana leaned against the man who would soon be her husband and sighed with contentment. She'd never known that being wrong could feel so right.

Chapter Twenty-Five

"Mom!" Jazmine slammed into the bathroom of Shana's old house in West Seattle, where Ali was preparing for work. They'd been living there for the last seven weeks, ever since her discharge from the Navy. Her life and that of her sister's had been a whirlwind for the past half year.

Once Shana and Adam had decided on marriage, their wedding had happened fast, but not quite as fast as originally planned. Fortunately—for the convenience of the guests—it had taken place in Seattle, not Hawaii. No sooner had Ali returned to San Diego in December than she boarded a plane to Washington for the wedding. From everything she heard, in phone calls and e-mails, Shana and Adam were blissfully happy and enjoying life in Honolulu.

At the end of her tour, Alison had left the *USS Wood-*

row Wilson and within a matter of weeks was released from her commitment to the Navy.

Because Shana had signed a lease on the rental house in Seattle, Ali was able to move there. Jazmine was back in the same school now and doing well. Ali liked Seattle and it was as good a place to settle as any.

The retired couple who'd purchased Shana's ice-cream and pizza parlor had been accommodating and helpful when Ali arrived in Seattle. They loved her daughter and she loved them, too.

"Mom," Jazmine repeated. "Do you remember what today is?"

As if anyone needed to remind her. "Yes, sweetheart, I remember."

"It's Dad's birthday—and it's the day you're meeting Commander Dillon." Apparently her daughter felt it was necessary to tell her, anyway. "What time?" she asked urgently.

"One o'clock in Pike Place Market." Alison had arranged a half day off before she'd been hired at West Seattle Hospital. Her hand shook as she brushed her hair. Frank and Alison talked nearly every day and sent e-mail messages when it wasn't possible to chat on the phone.

Because of Navy regulations, they'd controlled their growing attraction and their intense feelings for each other while they were aboard the carrier. But now that Alison had been officially discharged, they were free to explore those emotions, and to express them. Circumstances had made that challenging; Alison had moved to Seattle and Frank was stationed in San Diego with the *USS Woodrow Wilson*.

"He's going to ask you to marry him."

"Jazmine!" Overnight her daughter had turned into

a romance expert. Given the success of her matchmaking efforts with Shana and Adam, the girl was convinced she had an aptitude for this.

"Mom, Commander Dillon would be a fool not to marry you."

Frank and Jazmine routinely chatted via the Internet, too. Maybe her daughter knew something she didn't, but Alison doubted it.

"You're in love with him," Jazmine said with all the confidence of one who had insider information, "and he's crazy about you."

"Jazmine!"

"Yup, that's my name."

Alison put down her brush and inhaled a calming breath. "I'm very fond of Frank…. He's a wonderful man, but we barely know each other."

"I like him," her daughter said.

"I know and I like him, too."

"Like?" Jazmine scoffed and shook her head. "Who are you kidding? I don't understand adults. Every time I tell him he should marry you, Commander Dillon—"

"What?" Alison exploded, outraged that her daughter had this sort of conversation with Frank. Her face burned with mortification; she could only imagine what he must think.

"Don't go ballistic on me, Mom. You know Commander Dillon and I e-mail each other."

"Yes, but…"

"Okay, okay," Jazmine asserted, shaking her head as if she were losing her patience. "Here's the deal. You and Commander Dillon talk, and if you need me to sort anything out for you, just let me know. He's coming to dinner tonight, isn't he?"

"I invited him, but—"

"He'll be here." She kissed Alison on the cheek and added, "I've gotta go or I'll be late for the bus. Have a great day." With that Jazmine headed out of the bathroom. She grabbed her coat and backpack, and adjusted her hood against the January drizzle.

Alison followed her to the door and watched her daughter meet her friends and walk to the bus stop. Jazmine seemed utterly sure that this meeting with Frank would have a fairy-tale ending. Alison wished she shared her daughter's positive attitude. She was nervous and didn't mind admitting it.

In an effort to settle her nerves, Alison reached for the phone to call her sister. Remembering the time difference between the West Coast and Hawaii, she replaced it. Eight Seattle time was far too early to phone Shana and even if she reached her, Alison wouldn't know what to say.

By noon when she left the hospital and drove into downtown Seattle her stomach was in a state of chaos. Jazmine knew her far too well. Alison did love Frank. She had for months, and now they were finally meeting at the time and place they'd arranged last summer. Because she was no longer in the Navy, there were no official barriers between them. As for other kinds of obstacles… She didn't know.

After parking in a waterfront lot, Alison climbed the stairs up to Pike Place Market, coming in the back entrance. They'd agreed to meet at the figure of the bronze pig in front. Her heart pounded hard, but that had little to do with the flight of stairs she'd just climbed. A glance at her watch told her she was fifteen minutes early.

A part of her feared Frank wouldn't show. Shades of that old movie, *An Affair to Remember.*

It had started to rain and the sky was dark gray. This was an ominous sign as far as Alison was concerned. The fishmongers were busily arranging seafood on beds of crushed ice as tourists and shoppers crowded the aisles. With extra time on her hands, Alison could do a bit of shopping. But her nerves were stretched so tight she didn't think she was capable of doing anything more than standing next to the bronze pig.

To her surprise, Frank was already there, looking around anxiously. He seemed uncomfortable and unsure of himself, and almost immediately Ali's unease left her.

"Did you think I wouldn't come?" she asked softly, walking over to meet him.

From experience, Alison knew Frank wasn't a man who smiled often. But when he saw her, his face underwent a transformation and he broke into a wide grin.

Alison wasn't sure who moved first, but in the next moment, she was in his arms. They clung to each other for a long time. It would be completely out of character for him to kiss her in such a public place, and she accepted that.

"Have you had lunch?" he asked, as she reluctantly stepped out of his embrace.

"No, but there's a great chowder bar on the waterfront," she told him. As they held hands, she led him down the same path she'd recently taken from the parking area. She liked the feel of his hand in hers, and the way that simple action connected them.

They ordered fish and chips and ate outside under a large canopy on the wharf, protected from the elements. She felt too tense to be hungry. They talked very little.

"The ferry's coming in," Alison said and by unspoken agreement they walked to the end of the pier to watch it glide toward the dock.

Standing side by side, they gazed out over the choppy water of Puget Sound. After a few minutes, Frank placed an arm around her shoulders. Alison leaned against him, savoring this closeness to the man she loved.

Without warning, he turned her so that she faced him and then he kissed her. His mouth was gentle and she instinctively opened to him. Seconds later his hands were in her hair, bunching it as he slanted his lips over hers and his kiss grew more insistent.

With his arms around her, Frank rested his chin on her head. "I told myself I wouldn't do that," he said in a low voice. "Not here, not like this."

"I think I would've died if you hadn't," she whispered back.

"I'm no bargain, Alison."

"Stop."

"No, I mean it, but God help me, I love you and I know I'll love Jazmine, too."

Alison smiled softly. "She's eager to meet you in person."

His arms relaxed as he brushed his lips against her temple. "I have a week's leave, but then I have to head back to San Diego. It isn't much time to make an important decision, but I'm hoping that by the end of the week you'll know how you feel about me."

Alison didn't need any time; her decision was made.

"I know you loved Peter and that he's Jazmine's father," Frank continued.

"I'll always love Peter," Alison said.

"I want you to. He was your husband and he died serving his country. I respect him and I have no intention of replacing him in your life or Jazmine's."

"Frank, what are you saying?"

He inhaled harshly. "I was hoping, praying actually, that by the end of this week you might know your feelings well enough… What I mean is that I'd like you to be my wife."

"I don't need a week—"

"You do," he told her, "we both do." And he kissed her again with such abandon and joy that when he released her, Alison was convinced she'd rather be in his arms than breathe.

A week later, just before Frank was scheduled to return to San Diego, the three of them planned dinner together. While Alison flitted about the kitchen checking on their meal, Jazmine set the table.

Before they sat down to eat, Frank pulled two small boxes out of his pocket and ceremonially placed them on the table.

Alison was carrying a large green salad and nearly dropped the bowl when she saw the velvet cases.

Frank glanced at her with a mildly guilty look. "If you'd rather wait until after dinner, that's fine, but I know I'd enjoy the meal a lot more if I had your answer first."

"Do I get to choose between two rings?" she asked, wondering why he'd brought two boxes.

"No," he said. "There's a necklace in one of them for Jazmine."

Her daughter came out of the kitchen clutching three bottles of salad dressing. It didn't take her long to assess the situation. "The answer is yes," Jazmine stated matter-of-factly.

"Yes," Alison echoed, nodding vigorously.

Frank opened the first of the two velvet boxes and slipped the small single-pearl necklace around Jazmine's neck and fastened it. "I felt it was important that I make a promise to you, too," he said to Ali's daughter. "I wanted to assure you that I will love you. I plan to be a good stepfather and, most importantly, I vow to always love your mother."

Jazmine blinked back tears and so did Alison. "I'll wear it every day and I swear I'll never lose it." Frank hugged the child.

Then he opened the second box and took out a large solitaire diamond ring. While Alison tried not to weep, he slipped it onto her ring finger. He held her gaze, and in his eyes Alison saw his love and the promise he was making. "I love you," he whispered.

"I love you, too."

The doorbell chimed, and before Jazmine could race toward it, the door opened and Shana hurried into the house, Adam directly behind her. "We aren't too late, are we?" she asked, laughing and excited. "Frank's still here, isn't he?"

"Shana." Alison ran across the room to her sister and they threw their arms around each other.

Frank and Adam shook hands and introduced themselves.

"Actually, your timing's perfect," Alison told Shana, and with tears clouding her eyes, she thrust out her left hand so her sister could examine her engagement ring.

Shana squealed with joy and hugged Alison excitedly, then hugged her brother-in-law to be.

"How did you know?" Alison asked.

"We didn't," Adam answered. "We came because we have some exciting news of our own."

"We're pregnant," Shana burst out.

Now it was Alison's turn to shout with happiness.

"Can I babysit?" Jazmine asked. "I could spend the summers with you in Hawaii and—"

"We'll decide that later," Alison said, cutting her daughter off. "We were about to sit down for dinner. Join us," she insisted.

The two women immediately went into the kitchen. While Alison got out extra silverware, Shana took the dinner and salad plates from the cupboard, along with two extra water glasses. Jazmine promptly delivered them to the table.

Shana paused. "Less than a year ago who would've believed we'd both have Navy husbands?"

"Navy husbands," Alison repeated as her diamond flashed in the light. "It has a nice sound to it, doesn't it?"

"The nicest sound in the world," Shana agreed.

* * * * *

Look for Debbie Macomber's new novel,
The Shop on Blossom Street,
available in September 2006.

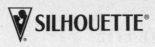 **SILHOUETTE®**

SPECIAL EDITION™

CABIN FEVER
by Karen Rose Smith

When handsome playboy Brad Vaughn and his beautiful secretary, Emily Stanton, are stranded in a blizzard in a cabin, it seems the inevitable will happen. But Emily plays for keeps and can she convince Brad that they share something really special?

DADDY PATROL
by Sharon De Vita

Sheriff and local coach Joe Marino received a letter from fatherless twin boys wanting to learn how to play baseball. Their mother, Mattie Maguire, warned them from getting too attached to Joe…but would she follow her own advice?

MIDNIGHT CRAVINGS
by Elizabeth Harbison

Sexy Chief of Police Dan Duvall was a man of few words. But then city-girl Josephine Ross strolled into his town and began stirring passions in him…

Don't miss out!
On sale from 18th August 2006

Available at WHSmith, Tesco, ASDA, Borders, Eason,
Sainsbury's and most bookshops
www.silhouette.co.uk

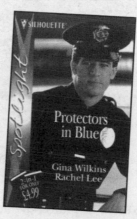

The child she loves…is his child.

And now he knows…

HER SISTER'S CHILDREN BY ROXANNE RUSTAND

When Claire Worth inherits her adorable but sad five-year-old twin nieces, their fourteen-year-old brother and a resort on Lake Superior, her life is turned upside down. Then Logan Matthews, her sister's sexy first husband turns up – will he want to break up Claire's fledgling family, when he discovers that Jason is his son?

WILD CAT AND THE MARINE BY JADE TAYLOR

One night of passion doesn't make a marriage, but it could make a child. A beautiful daughter. Cat Darnell hadn't been able to trample on her lover's dream and kept her secret. Joey was the light of her life. And now, finally, Jackson Gray was coming home…was going to meet his little girl…

On sale 4th August 2006

"I was fifteen when my mother finally told me the truth about my father. She didn't mean to. She meant to keep it a secret forever. If she'd succeeded it might have saved us all."

When a hauntingly familiar stranger knocks on Roberta Dutreau's door, she is compelled to begin a journey of self-discovery leading back to her childhood. But is she ready to know the truth about what happened to her, her best friend Cynthia and their mothers that tragic night ten years ago?

16th June 2006

MIRA

FREE

4 BOOKS AND A SURPRISE GIFT!

We would like to take this opportunity to thank you for reading this Silhouette® book by offering you the chance to take FOUR more specially selected titles from the Special Edition™ series absolutely FREE! We're also making this offer to introduce you to the benefits of the Mills & Boon® Reader Service™—

- ★ **FREE home delivery**
- ★ **FREE gifts and competitions**
- ★ **FREE monthly Newsletter**
- ★ **Books available before they're in the shops**
- ★ **Exclusive Reader Service offers**

Accepting these FREE books and gift places you under no obligation to buy; you may cancel at any time, even after receiving your free shipment. Simply complete your details below and return the entire page to the address below. You don't even need a stamp!

YES! Please send me 4 free Special Edition books and a surprise gift. I understand that unless you hear from me, I will receive 6 superb new titles every month for just £3.10 each, postage and packing free. I am under no obligation to purchase any books and may cancel my subscription at any time. The free books and gift will be mine to keep in any case.

E6ZEE

Ms/Mrs/Miss/Mr...Initials ....
BLOCK CAPITALS PLEASE

Surname ....

Address ....

....

....Postcode ....

Send this whole page to:
The Reader Service, FREEPOST CN81, Croydon, CR9 3WZ